ONE MAN'S VALOR

Leo Baeck and the Holocaust

‹

JEWISH BIOGRAPHY SERIES

Anne E. Neimark

ONE MAN'S VALOR

Leo Baeck and the Holocaust

illustrated with photographs

LODESTAR BOOKS   E. P. Dutton   New York

The author and publisher gratefully acknowledge permission to reprint the photographs in this book, as follows:

on pages 38 and 62, courtesy of Marianne Berlak Dreyfus

on pages 45 and 57 (bottom), courtesy of Landesbild-stelle Berlin

all other photographs, courtesy of the Leo Baeck Institute

Library of Congress Cataloging in Publication Data

Neimark, Anne E.
One man's valor.

(Jewish biography series)
"Lodestar books."
Bibliography: p.
Includes index.
Summary: Relates the story of a German Jew who became a great rabbi and national spiritual leader and fought courageously against the persecution of his people during the Nazi years.
1. Baeck, Leo, 1873–1956—Juvenile literature.
2. Rabbis—Germany—Biography—Juvenile literature.
3. Holocaust, Jewish (1939–1945)—Germany—Juvenile literature. 4. Terezín (Czechoslovakia: Concentration camp)—Juvenile literature. [1. Baeck, Leo, 1873–1956.
2. Rabbis. 3. Holocaust, Jewish (1939–1945)—Germany]
I. Title. II. Series.
BM755.B32N45 1986 296.3'092'4 [B] [92] 85-27366
ISBN 0-525-67175-7

Published in the United States by E. P. Dutton,
2 Park Avenue, New York, N.Y. 10016

Published simultaneously in Canada by
Fitzhenry & Whiteside Limited, Toronto

Editor: Virginia Buckley

Printed in the U.S.A.   COBE   First Edition
10 9 8 7 6 5 4 3 2 1

To my friend Bill DeWoskin—
who spoke of history and heritage

Contents

Acknowledgments

My thanks to Marianne Berlak Dreyfus for her insights and recollections concerning her grandfather, Rabbi Leo Baeck—and to Vivian Singer for her hours of instruction in Jewish theology.

1

To Be a Jew

Graduation night of 1890 had come at last. In the Gymnasium school of Lissa, Germany, only a few Jewish boys had been allowed as students among the Christians. One of them, seventeen-year-old Leo Baeck, was valedictorian. Dressed in a dark cutaway coat that seemed strangely large for his thin, angular frame, he waited on stage with his classmates.

In the auditorium below, Leo's ten sisters and brothers were seated behind his parents. His father, the Rabbi Samuel Bäck, had been nodding at townspeople who stopped to give greeting. For Leo, being the son of a rabbi was both a wonderment and a duty. He, too, had decided to join the rabbinate. He wanted to honor his name, which had been modernized from Bäck to Baeck. He wanted to please his father.

Straightening the lapels of his coat, he remembered not to bend forward. Would anyone know what was hidden under the coat? Would he seem foolish on this night?

1

He watched the headmaster of the Gymnasium carry the graduation certificates to a wooden podium. Before roll call began, Leo would be asked to give his valedictory speech. He must, as he'd promised himself, keep his spine stiff as a rod, hold everything in place. He must concentrate on his words. Ever since he'd begun to study Talmud, the sweetness of the words symbolized by a drop of honey placed on the first page set before him, words had become a refuge.

Ten times that morning he had practiced his speech, though it wasn't the speech that worried him. Before the sky had lightened, while the coat hung in his closet, he'd sat on the steps of the synagogue. An apple nestled in his pocket; sentences bloomed inside his head. Three of the elders, the old and Orthodox Jews, had shuffled by under wide-brimmed hats. Whenever the elders saw Leo, they tried persuading him to take rabbinical training in Lissa, not in Breslau or Berlin. "We must keep our covenant with God," they'd tell him. "We are His Chosen People. Stay where you belong, Leo. In Breslau, in Berlin, too much corrupts."

Sometimes Leo reminded the elders that his own father, the Rabbi Bäck, had dared acquire a philosophy degree at the University of Vienna. But the morning of graduation, Leo was silent about his future. Walking quickly from the synagogue, he'd crisscrossed the streets of Lissa, where Jews lived apart from Catholics and Protestants—as Jews always lived apart from those who shunned them. His speech, practiced aloud, caused no one's notice. Jews were accustomed to sounds. Weren't prayers and psalms chanted daily in synagogue? Didn't the *shofar*, or ram's horn, blow for most of the month of Elul and on Rosh Hashanah, the start of the Jewish New Year? And in parlors and vestibules, storefronts and rear rooms, Lissa's Jews read aloud from Torah—part of the Old Testament—or from Talmud, the immense written record of Jewish law, ritual, and ethics.

Now, in the auditorium, Leo was dressed for graduation. Nothing more could be done about the coat. A rabbi's family, he reassured himself, was frequently poor. Though his father wrote textbooks, the money he earned was for education, not for finery or frills. Most of Lissa's Jews were simple merchants or peddlers, just scraping by. To escape the drabness, some joined the Prussian army, leaving on the railway that had opened nearby when Leo was five. Christian businessmen praised the train, but to Leo it had seemed a *golem*, a manlike creature out of Hebrew legend, belching fire.

The headmaster of the Gymnasium nodded. From the podium, Leo stared down at his family, watching his mother, Eva, proudly smooth out her dress. One of his sisters was giggling. Slowly, he began to thank the faculty in behalf of his class. His sentences came almost as easily to him as morning prayer. Arms straight at his sides, head poised at center, he felt as if he were reciting the eighteen benedictions.

What matter, he asked himself, if the coat had its secrets? What difference that other valedictorians, especially Christian valedictorians, were fitted by tailors for new coats? His father's cutaway coat had been retrieved from an old, dusty traveling trunk for him to borrow. It had hung on his shoulders in giant gnarls of cloth matched to Samuel Bäck's wider girth, but his mother was not dissuaded. Leo was best in his class; he should, as the headmaster said, be valedictorian. Enlisting the family's help, his mother had stuffed stocking balls, cotton-soft, into the coat's shoulders.

Leo took a deep breath, nearing the midpoint of his speech. The miracle of knowledge had been his subject: the art of teaching, the gift of learning. In the audience, he saw three of the Orthodox elders. Forgetting his rigid posture, he leaned forward, hoping they would understand that even if he went away to study wonders, he would never forsake them.

Suddenly, as he swung his hand forward, something loosened at Leo's shoulder. Startled, he felt a bulge slip down the length of his left sleeve. His heart pounded, and in a desperate lurch he managed to twist his hand quickly enough to catch the white stocking ball that, secret no longer, had lost its moorings and popped out of his cuff for everyone to see.

A gasp and some laughter rose from the audience. Peering out past the faces of the townspeople, Leo located the shape of his father's head, the dark of his father's eyes. What now, Papa? he wanted to ask. Would the Christian boys tell him later that Jews were aligned with the devil and deserved punishment from the true God?

Samuel Bäck, however, appeared only to be waiting for his son to continue the valedictory speech. Sitting erect among both Christians and Jews, his gaze was patient, unwavering. Leo wrestled with a silence that had fastened onto his next sentence. Part of him yearned to run from the stage, to fling off the coat with the bulky shoulders and floppy sleeves, to let the rest of the stocking balls scatter. Yet he saw in his memory the volcanic train of his childhood on its journey past Lissa, saw himself at the age of five wanting to run from the fiery *golem*.

He had not run at all. He had let the sounds of train thunder pass through him. Nor would he run now. No matter how foolish he looked, stocking ball in hand, his valedictory speech must be finished. He would find his sentences, pluck out the mantle of his words, and *stay*.

When had he discovered, Leo often wondered, what it meant to be a Jew? Riding with his father on wagon trips over the German countryside before he'd entered the Gymnasium, he had heard many tales. The Jews, said Samuel Bäck, settled in the land of Palestine—called also Canaan, Zion, or Israel—in 1200 B.C. Jews believed in one God who'd revealed Himself to Abraham, the first Jew. A covenant was made: The Jews must follow God's Law, or Commandments; in return, they would be the Chosen People, promised the land of Canaan. As Jews grew in number, God's Law had grown. It became Torah, the first five biblical books; it became the Prophetic Writings.

Scrolls of Torah, explained Samuel Bäck, were carried by early Jews in a Holy Ark. David, second king of the Jews, rescued the Ark from enemies. Solomon, the third king, built the Temple in Jerusalem, the sacred capital of Palestine, to house the Ark. Priests presided in the Temple, while prophets warned of sins or sang of justice.

Leo's dreams had been filled with images of priests, kings, and prophets, those stalwart warriors of deed and spirit. Rabbis, he learned, were the teachers and translators of God's Law. His father's own father, Nathan, and grandfather, Abraham Bäck, had been rabbis; the name Bäck meant son of a pious man or martyr. But why, Leo had asked his father, had Jews fallen into suffering?

How the stories had multiplied! Other peoples, said Samuel Bäck, invaded tiny Palestine; sometimes the Jews were conquered. They lived as slaves in Egypt, were captives in Babylonia, Assyria, Persia, ancient Greece. When Palestine was lost to the Roman Empire, Jews wandered the earth ever after among alien nations. They were traded, slaughtered, driven from solace, yet they endured. Christianity, born of their ranks, competed with them for converts, abandoned Torah for the worship of Jesus Christ, and became state religion of ancient Rome—but this, too, Jews survived.

Weeks before his thirteenth birthday, in a ceremony of tradition at Lissa's synagogue, Leo had become a Bar Mitzvah, a Jewish "man of duty." Torah and Talmud were sweeter to him than the air he breathed. At the Gymnasium school, he'd made one or two friends among Christian students. When the others snubbed him, he asked, "Wasn't Jesus Christ born a Jew? Shouldn't Christians and Jews be brothers?"

The replies left him knowing more of what it meant to be a Jew. "Didn't Jews," asked his classmates, "deliver Jesus Christ to the Romans for crucifying?"

"Most Jews," Leo answered, "rallied to protect Jesus from the Romans. They wept at his Crucifixion."

"Don't Jews," said his classmates, "mix the blood of

Christians into unleavened bread for their Passover holiday? Didn't they cause the Black Death, the bubonic plague?
Or a year of drought in Vienna? Or epidemics of leprosy?"

"No!" Leo had shouted. "Where do you hear such lies?"
But he'd seen how even great Jewish writers and philoso-
phers—Spinoza, Saadia, Maimonides, Moses Mendels-
sohn—had not erased the world's hatreds. If Jews wandered, so must they still search: for truth, for strength, for
the scepter of justice.

Ripening in him, then, was his life decision—but when,
exactly, had it been sown? It must have dawned at some
moment he could not name—perhaps after his Bar Mitzvah
or in the year of his valedictory speech at the Gymnasium
school. His brothers might travel other paths, but he—like
his father, grandfather, and great-grandfather before him—
would pledge his life to the rabbinate, become a teacher of
Judaism.

On the night of his graduation in Lissa, his speech completed and certificate issued, he'd walked home from the
Gymnasium in his father's coat, the stocking balls stuffed
into the ample pockets. History was on his mind, but so were
enlightenment and change. Being a Jew, Leo told himself,
was a story, an astonishment that, from the very beginnings, had been without end.

2

Changing Times

Leo studied first in Breslau, then in Berlin. To him, the cities had been warnings whispered by Lissa's elders. Now he saw for himself. Petitions might circulate against Jews, but no longer were their tongues cut out and sewn to their clothes. Jewish communities, in fact, had grown. For three years, Leo was enrolled at a rabbinical seminary in Breslau. In 1894, he was admitted to Berlin's scholarly Hochschule seminary and to graduate work at the university.

He'd pleaded with his father to let him go to Berlin. The Jews, he explained, numbered ninety thousand in the capital city. Some were allowed to enter law, medicine, the arts. They had built schools and charity houses; their synagogues shone with tinted glass.

"Go," said Samuel Bäck. "Tuition is put away for you. But remember, Leo, you are a poor Jewish student. If Berlin dazzles you too much, you'll ache instead of learn."

What dazzled Leo in Berlin was the abundance of infor-

Leo studied for three years at the Hochschule seminary in Berlin.

mation. Books were sold on the mile-long promenade along avenue Unter den Linden; newspapers fluttered from the lobbies of hotels. The stores hung posters of the State Opera House, the museums, the great trade fair planned for

1896. From his first day in Berlin, Leo attended lectures. At the university, he studied literature, philosophy, and language. At the Hochschule were classes in Talmud; comparative religion; homiletics, or the art of preaching; and *midrash*, the ancient commentaries on Jewish scripture.

His longing to understand was like a drum sound inside him. He had learned to read Greek, Latin, and English, as well as Aramaic, Hebrew, and Yiddish. In his rented room in Berlin's working-class district, he sat up nights with books, reading until dawn, when he would recite morning prayer. Then, bleary-eyed student became believer. Wearing his *tallis*, or prayer shawl, he'd strap two tiny leather *tefillin* boxes containing biblical verses to his left arm and forehead. "Joy is ours," he'd begin, the ancient ritual regained. "How good is our portion; how lovely is our heritage."

Leo had memorized the Hebrew prayer book. He could repeat countless pages of Torah and Talmud. Yet he couldn't afford to buy the books he had come to Berlin to read. Other students gathered in the shops; he dashed from library to library, adding his name to waiting lists or checking to see what was in the stacks. Sometimes he borrowed a book from a classmate, handling it like a treasure that was his for a day.

Winters in Berlin were cold, and Leo warmed himself in the coffeehouses, his class notes spread over a bench or chair. One cup of coffee might bring him a free doughnut, and he could collect hardened wax leavings from table candles to make lights for his room. A future rabbi, he told himself, did not need a full stomach or store-bought candles or a new coat. Better to know Torah and Talmud backward and forward; for that, a little hunger was a small price to pay.

One evening, however, Leo was especially hungry. He was in his second year in Berlin, and his trousers were loose on him. He counted the money in his pocket; enough for a soft-boiled egg at an outdoor café. Putting aside the book he'd been reading, he went out into the street. Two bearded Jews greeted him, heads covered by yarmulke caps. The Orthodox Jews, strict in their behavior like his own family, had kept their traditional dress and long sidecurls of hair, but in letters home Leo mentioned how Liberal Jews were dressing like Christians. "A shame on their houses!" he could almost hear the elders scold. "Jews who read Torah in German, not Hebrew? Soon they will be pagans!"

Near the Ringbahn, Berlin's inner-city railway, Leo came upon a small crowd. An organ-grinder and a monkey were performing on a slatted platform. Stopping, Leo watched the animal tip its red hat for coins. His stomach knotted in hunger, but the monkey cocked its head and grinned at him. Impulsively, he reached into his pocket—visions of food disappearing—to find a coin. His fingers groped downward against the cloth lining, pushed sideways onto the stitching, but to his surprise his pocket was empty.

A shuffling nearby turned out to be a man waving a large knapsack upside down in the air. "Pickpocket!" the man shouted. "Pickpocket!" Suddenly two women screamed. Protectively, the organ-grinder grabbed the monkey in his arms. A street robbery, Leo thought, but with half-hearted hope he searched his other pockets. They, too, were empty, and he stood motionless on the street. He'd have to use rent money for food, ask his landlord to permit him extra days until funds could be sent from home. What if Herr Bringle said no?

At last, Leo turned to follow the Ringbahn back toward his rented room. The pickpocket must have escaped down an alley or into the arbor of a park. Several policemen arrived, climbing onto the organ-grinder's platform, hawking for witnesses, but the crowd had dispersed, and no one came forward.

Leo was at a corner when he heard the voice of the man with the knapsack. "A Jew!" the man sneered to a companion. "It must have been a Jew! Who else would rob us blind?" Tempted to answer, to defend against injustice as he had at the Gymnasium school, Leo said nothing. Shivering slightly, he hastened across the street. Jews had improved their lot in Berlin, and in Germany itself, but persecutions still hounded his people. Even while Christians and Jews lived more in accord, deputies who called themselves anti-Semites, haters of Jews, had been elected to the Reichstag, Germany's governing body.

In ten months, Leo counted, his Hochschule training would be finished; he would be ordained a rabbi. Somewhere he would find employment at a synagogue. He hoped, also, to write of Judaism. But until a congregation hired him, he would tackle Berlin as a poor Jewish student.

Ten months. The challenge of helping sanctify his religion, of working for acceptance of Jews among non-Jews, was before him. On the stairway to his room, the number ten fell into a kind of chant inside his mind. Ten were the Commandments, he uttered to himself, given to Moses by God. Ten were the days of penitence between the Holy Days of Rosh Hashanah and Yom Kippur. Ten were the generations between Adam and Noah, Noah and Abraham.

And ten, Leo would have liked to tell the man who'd accused a Jew of robbing his knapsack, were the tests of faith undergone by Abraham, the very first Jew.

Ordination in May 1897 brought Leo inquiries from two German synagogues, neither in Berlin. Rabbinical posts were scarce. Finally his application was accepted in Oppeln, an east German city of 30,000 with 750 Jews, a few hours' wagon ride from Lissa. By June, he'd settled in that city, becoming the rabbi to dedicate its new synagogue. His first meeting with his congregants was outside the synagogue gate on the morning of dedication.

Samuel and Eva Bäck had traveled from Lissa for the celebrating. At sunrise, Leo and his father hiked along the outskirts of Oppeln's market square. In the distance was the Oder River and a pond used for winter skating. Samuel Bäck eyed his son as carefully as had the synagogue board. A responsibility was being bestowed: father to son, rabbi to rabbi. Would Leo be worthy? was the question.

The young rabbi

At the synagogue, Leo blessed his congregants and the building they would occupy. The key to the front door was squeezed tightly in his hand as he led everyone in prayer. "Dear God," he said, "you are our protection forever and ever. Before the mountains came and the earth and the world were created, you were God eternally and eternally."

A center of stillness lay in the sanctuary of the brick building. Though Leo missed Berlin, familiar sights eased him. Across the Diaspora, the wide scattering of Jewish communities beyond Palestine, Jews recreated their historic symbols. On the *bimah,* or platform, of the Oppeln synagogue, an Ark held the scrolls of Torah. In front of the Ark burned an eternal light to signify the abiding God. These were measures, Leo would write, to honor "holy words in a holy room."

Essays Leo had composed in Berlin were printed in German journals. He'd written of orthodoxy—belief in established ritual—and of liberalism—belief in reform. The past, he said, was valuable where it enriched the present, but new ideas should be considered. In Oppeln, months after the dedication, he introduced a choir and an organ into the synagogue. Orthodox congregants angrily objected. Keyboard instruments, they said, were popular in Christian churches, not in traditional synagogues. "Times change," he told them gently, "and we change in them."

Choir and organ music became a source of pride to the congregation. Leo's daily habits as a young rabbi—devotion to prayer and strapping on of *tefillin*—appeased his Orthodox members. He satisfied Liberals by combining synagogue ritual with further reform. Yet he learned he could not always make peace. In 1898, a year after coming to Oppeln, he was invited to a Berlin meeting of ninety-four German rabbis. The youngest of the group, the one with the least experience, he rashly opposed his colleagues and put his reputation at risk.

At the meeting hall in Berlin, a vote was scheduled to censure the new Jewish movement, Zionism, that urged Jews to avoid European persecution by reclaiming Palestine. Sitting in wide rows of chairs, the convening rabbis pointed to inroads made by Jews into German culture. Germany, they agreed, gradually was becoming a home to its Jews. Why antagonize some German Christians by threatening to leave? Why anger Turks, Moslems, Arabs, and Christians occupying modern Palestine by fighting them over land?

Leo was not a Zionist, but he rose to his feet in protest. He could not, he said, support any vote denying Zionists a hearing. He did not wish to be estranged from Germany; he considered himself a German citizen as well as a Jew. But why should the new idea, Zionism, be outlawed? Who could ignore the League of Anti-Semitism functioning in Berlin? Who could forget the recent killing raids, the pogroms, causing thousands of Russian Jews to flee for their lives? Couldn't a pogrom in Russia become a pogrom in Germany?

The rabbis had twisted in their seats to look at Leo in horror. Such an upstart, their expressions seemed to say. Was this the son of Samuel Bäck? How dare he give opposition!

But Leo did not stop talking. Someday, he said, the children and grandchildren of the rabbis in the meeting hall might need a homeland. Zionists wanted to make certain that Palestine awaited them.

Glaring, the presiding rabbi struck a gavel on a tabletop, demanding the deciding vote. Those in favor of censure were to raise their hands. Reluctantly, Leo waited. A thick forest surrounded him as more than ninety rabbis lifted their arms above their heads. Outside, on the street called Potsdammerstrasse, tour buses clattered past the window. Leo recalled walking the street as a student, library book under his arm, a precious wedge of cheese in a bag. Yet he was no longer that student. Other concerns beckoned him.

Once more the gavel struck the table. If anyone, the presiding rabbi muttered, chose to vote against censure, would that person please raise his hand? Stretching forward, face flushed, Leo slowly lifted both hands in the air. He felt he was in isolation in the room. No one acknowledged his presence. Papers were shuffled, and someone coughed. A sigh of disgust wheezed behind him.

In moments, after the vote was tabulated for Berlin newspapers, the meeting was abruptly adjourned. Ninety-three black-suited rabbis filed down the aisles, heads shaking in disapproval over Leo Baeck's defection. Leo knew he must return to Oppeln to face questions from his congregation. He hoped his vote would not upset them. His colleagues, however, had been unapproachable. As they pushed past him in the hall, he almost reached out to tap an elbow or two. Could he have been more convincing to them? The rabbis rejected Zionism in fear of reprisals from German Christians, out of desire for welcome in German cities and towns. Yet he could not disregard the Zionist call or the stirrings of danger that trailed Jews like a shroud.

Walking into the Berlin air, whorls of afternoon shadows dappling the street, Leo heard the pealing of church bells, and he glanced up at a tapering spire. Change, he was learning—whether a keyboard and choir in synagogue or tolerance among peoples—must be carefully taught. Dark days of destruction had afflicted the Jews before. How could anyone promise that such days would not come again?

3

A Rabbi and a Scholar

Past sundown each Friday, the start of the Jewish Sabbath, Oppeln's synagogue filled with congregants. The Sabbath, or *Shabbos*, was a time of rest and reflection, hallowed until sundown on Saturday. According to tradition, certain labors were forbidden; harmony between man and nature was not to be disturbed. So Jews of Oppeln walked, rather than rode, to *Shabbos* services. Leo greeted them in the sanctuary, rabbinical robes brushing the tips of his shoes, *tallis* draped over his shoulders.

From his first *Shabbos* in Oppeln, he'd noticed a dark-eyed young woman intently following his sermon. She was Natalie Hamburger, granddaughter of a former rabbi of the community. On Fridays, Leo arrived at the sanctuary well before sundown. Candles soon would flare, prayer books, or *siddurs*, would be open, but something more than Sabbath joy prompted his pacing on the *bimah*. As when he was a student in Lissa, he practiced his words. At the end of each

16

Friday sermon, he allowed himself a glance at Natalie Hamburger. If she smiled at him, he was content.

On two Sundays, overcoming his shyness toward her, Leo invited Natalie to take a stroll. He talked to her of the religious class he'd begun teaching in secular school and of the students who gathered in his small apartment on Saturdays for discussions and for Sabbath cakes and tea. Natalie's smile seemed warmer than the October sun. She told him of the children at services who basked in "the Rabbi Baeck's kindness."

The Sunday strolls became a fixture in Oppeln. Natalie was tall and gracious; townspeople said she complemented the young rabbi of "new ideas." Leo, too, liked her at his side. When he'd returned from the vote on Zionism in Berlin, she had calmed him. Gradually, his thoughts of her turned more serious. While performing weddings at the synagogue, he imagined himself the groom and Natalie the bride. Would their names, he wondered, ever grace a *ketubah*, the marriage contract?

In 1899, two years after they'd met, Leo and Natalie were married in the synagogue of Oppeln. Relatives gathered for the ceremony and congregants presented rabbi and wife with a monogrammed silver chest. Natalie moved into Leo's apartment. His Saturday gatherings of students were all the livelier with her home-baked cakes and embroidered chair cushions.

In a year, Natalie Baeck gave birth to a daughter who was named Ruth. Leo was twenty-seven years old. His thankfulness for the child deepened his bonds with the wider family of his congregation. If sometimes congregants questioned him, they also gave him their trust. He was arbiter of their fears and sorrows, their hopes and disappointments, their pleasures and regrets. "At your own Bar Mitzvah," Samuel Bäck said on a visit to Oppeln, "you were a man, Leo, in the eyes of Judaism. Now you are a man also among men."

The parlor of the apartment where Leo and Natalie lived was lined with shelves of books. Leo hadn't forgotten his poverty in Berlin; he lent his books to students. He himself never ceased being student or scholar. At five each morning, he memorized the classic literature of Greece, Rome, India, and China. He composed religious essays, which were published in the *Monatsschrift*, the most scholarly Jewish journal. He reviewed theologian Adolf von Harnack's *The Essence of Christianity*, a book critical of Jews.

Von Harnack's book had angered Leo. Never was Judaism dismissed with such arbitrary lies. Torah, said von Harnack, had been stolen by Jews and belonged "now and evermore to none but Christians." Judaism, the author stated, had "fallen under the sway of the devil" and was an "inferior, wrecked religion."

Leo wrote in his review that the Jewish minority survived in the midst of the Christian majority. Christianity, he said, stressed the worship of Christ, the rewards to be found in an afterlife, and the revelation of miracles. Judaism, however, preached the obligation to do God's will on earth, to pursue the moral task or deed, and to practice both faith and action. Jews had not stolen Torah; they were chosen to receive it. Nor were they wrecked or inferior. *So long as Judaism exists,* Leo wrote, *nobody will be able to say that the soul of man has surrendered. Its very existence through the ages is proof that conviction cannot be mastered by numbers.*

Leo's answers to von Harnack were compiled into his own book, *The Essence of Judaism,* by a German publisher. A bold counterpoint to *The Essence of Christianity*, the 1905 edition, which was later expanded in 1922, pitted the young rabbi of Oppeln against the Christian theologian. European Jews embraced Leo's book. Its message convinced them that Jews might share an equal place alongside Christians.

Whatever doubts over Samuel Bäck's son had been raised among the rabbis in Berlin were replaced with admiration. The upstart had become a model. To a Jew, scholarship was priceless. It enabled the reading of Torah. "Have you studied the Rabbi Leo Baeck?" Jewish mothers in Europe began asking their children. "Look what he has written! You, too, might someday write with such pride of the Jews."

In 1907, the Jewish community of Düsseldorf asked Leo to be its rabbi. This western city contained nearly three thousand Jews in a total population of two hundred sixty thousand. Leo and Natalie would miss Oppeln, but they accepted the offer. The Jews of Oppeln wept unashamedly during Leo's last sermon. Though he never used the word *I* in his sermons, this time he made an exception. He was grateful, he said, for the community "in which I, accompanied by an always growing benevolence, was listened to with openness." A rabbi, he told the families who'd become his friends, should never feel superior to his congregants. "Steps lead to the pulpit," he said, "yet they are only steps of wood or stone. They do not lead above the community."

Leo, Natalie, and seven-year-old Ruth moved to an apartment in Düsseldorf. In the excitement of unpacking, they ignored an anti-Jewish letter left on their doorstep.

Düsseldorf was in the Rhineland of western Germany and had a separate language style. Young people at services laughed at the unfamiliar rhythms in Leo's voice, but after several weeks he'd won them over. Teaching religious study, he used his own method of instruction. He added question-and-answer sessions to his lectures. Students could ask him anything; he would answer respectfully. Soon, young Jews of Düsseldorf realized that the rabbi with the strange accent—the one who'd written a famous book—never talked down to them.

Members of the Baeck family visited Düsseldorf. Some of Leo's sisters and brothers had married, and their children were old enough to travel by train to Uncle Leo's apartment. Ruth took her cousins hiking along the Rhine River. She showed them the synagogue in the distance, pointing to its green copper tower. Her papa, she'd boast to female cousins, was letting girls as well as boys graduate from religious class.

In the foreground: Leo Baeck's parents, Samuel and Eva Bäck, in 1907

Five years passed during Leo's post at the synagogue. Gratefully, he heard of fewer incidents of violence toward Jews. A period of relative calm had settled over Germany. Yet sometimes, late at night, Leo would awaken with a start, as if ominous murmurs had begun in the land, an eerie wailing or lament. Stirring the darkness beyond the slope of Natalie's arm was an apparition of something inhuman. He caught sight of a shape, some monstrous creature with groping tentacles and teeth. Yet watching Natalie sleep, he'd shake off the imprint of sights and sounds. Only a night-mare, he'd tell himself, smoothing the bed pillow of creases.

In 1912, Leo again moved his family, leaving Düsseldorf for Berlin. Sixteen years past his training there, he was hired by Berlin's Jewish community to serve various pulpits. The Rabbi Baeck, said a Jewish journal, had "entered the prominent rank of representatives and heralds of our religion." Such an important man belonged in Europe's most prestigious city.

Leo was still dazzled by Berlin. He rewalked the marble halls of the university and the vast street squares with their baroque cathedrals. At the Hochschule, he visited his former professors, attending a lecture in *midrash*. On two consecutive days, he went to see the latest synagogues of Berlin, astonished by their size and opulence. Outside the newly built Fasanenstrasse Synagogue, named for its *strasse*, or street, location, he craned his neck to take in the tops of three Moorish-style domes. Congregants gathered on the steps in swallowtail coats or silk dresses. Prayer books were printed partly in German. Had the Jews, Leo wondered, overcome their history of suffering? Why did a shudder tumble through him?

For a half hour, Leo stood before the grandeur of the Levetzowstrasse Synagogue, walking then to the vaulted entrance of a synagogue on Oranienburgerstrasse. Inside its doors, he stood in a majestic center aisle, flanked by enough benches to hold two thousand Jews. Series of windows curved about the light that glowed inward to the Ark. He found himself quietly reciting the *Shema*, the most sacred prayer of Judaism. "Hear, O Israel," he said, "the Lord our God, the Lord is One."

Love, confusion, and worry mixed in him. The splendor of the synagogues wrestled with his doubts. What was true? he asked. What was false? Were the Jews safe in Germany, or should the Zionists still call their brethren to Palestine? Were the synagogues built on shifting sands, or had the ancient slavery of Jews now become a dawn of solace? From scripture he'd memorized, Leo distinctly heard the eighth verse of the thirty-second Psalm. "I will instruct thee and teach thee," came God's words, "in the way which thou shalt go: I will guide thee with mine eye."

4

Outwitting Death

German children often played games of war. Strutting in army boots, balancing "rifle" sticks on shoulders, shouting formation commands, they imitated what they saw—Germany's love of military power. Imperial knights had ruled Germany into the nineteenth century. The Empire's first chancellor, Otto von Bismarck, believed in blood and iron. Germany's destiny, Bismarck said in 1871, was to conquer; its highest duty to increase its might.

In 1914, German hunger for battle led to the outbreak of World War I. On July 31, in Forum Fredericianum square in Berlin, army officers announced the mobilization of troops against France and Russia. Leo, Natalie, and Ruth were returning from a three-day vacation in Grunewald forest, southwest of the city. Scarcely were they home before Leo heard noise in the streets. Cries of *"Deutschland über alles!"*— "Germany above all else!"—echoed from rooftops.

Many Jews would see the war as a chance to prove allegiance to Germany. If they fought for the fatherland, mightn't they further close the gap between German Christian and German Jew? If they wore German uniforms, wouldn't they truly be countrymen? The first civil-service deputy enlisting in the German army was a Jew, Ludwig Frank, killed in battle within a year. The youngest volunteer was a thirteen-year-old Jewish boy, Joseph Zippes, who lost both legs in the war.

Leo was saddened by the arrival of World War I—so many lives would be in jeopardy. The desperate patriotism of Jewish soldiers made them especially vulnerable. But Leo, too, would serve the country of his birth. He volunteered as a *Feldrabbiner*, the Jewish equivalent of army chaplain. Though he'd been preaching in the Berlin synagogues whose grandeur disturbed him, and teaching *midrash* and homiletics at the Hochschule, he would leave family and peacetime activities waiting behind. On September 13, 1914, he kissed Natalie and Ruth good-bye and traveled for a week by train and wagon to the headquarters of the First German Army in France.

The war brought him into contact with Jewish soldiers of Russia and France. These men fought on the enemy side, but Leo could not deny a mutual kinship. In foxholes, in forests, on hilltops, he prayed with wounded or dying German Jews, but he never refused comfort to a Jew in foreign uniform. Each day, he moved to new battle zones, visiting field hospitals or crawling through trenches. *I spoke to your son,* he wrote to the anxious parents of a hospitalized Jewish soldier. *Our visit reminded him a bit of home, and his hopes were lifted.*

On High Holy Days, Leo insisted on conducting services. Gunfire crackling past him, he'd search out a haven—a rusty tank; a field with tree stumps for seats; a bombed-out, roofless church. Pale-faced Jewish soliders, blood-spattered and muddy, prayed alongside him. Rabbi and worshipers recited prayers for Rosh Hashanah, the New Year, or for Yom Kippur, the most solemn Jewish day of atonement.

A loyal German, Leo volunteered to serve as a military chaplain in World War I.

Leo urged the soldiers to strive for peace. *Das Gebot*, he said—the Commandment—was to do God's work. In the midst of war battles, he'd been seeking a personal peace. Samuel Bäck, in whose eyes he had found such wisdom, was suddenly dead. Granted temporary leave, the son offered traditional *Kaddish* prayer over his father's grave—his mother, sisters, and brothers looking to him for guidance. He assured them all that the spirit of Samuel Bäck was eternal, that even in death was renewal. But there were so many new questions he'd longed to ask his father. Now his deepest dialogues would be solely with God.

Death grew even closer in August of 1915. Traveling on the eastern and western fronts, Leo had frequently ridden by horse. One late afternoon, hot and thirsty, he stopped at a waterhole to refresh himself and to read letters from Natalie and Ruth. He had sent Ruth a special note for her fifteenth birthday, promising a gift on his next furlough—a flower vase made from a French cartridge shell. Tucking her thank-you into his jacket and reading Natalie's news of visits from two Oppeln students, he walked to the edge of the waterhole where his horse was tied. The animal had not cooled. Bubbles of froth and sweat, half-dried from the journey, oozed at its mouth.

Leo patted the horse's mane and pushed the warm head down toward the water. "Drink," he said, kneeling on a stone slab to cup his own hands in the green liquid. The horse neighed wildly. Rearing up on its hind legs, it startled Leo into letting the water run through his fingers. Terror blazed at him from the horse's oval eyes. Relying on a hunch, believing the animal might have some unerring knowledge, he determined that both he and his mount should drink elsewhere.

The next week, Leo learned that the waterhole in Germany had been poisoned by Russian troops. His horse had saved his life. In years to come, he would repeat the story of his judicious horse. Death, he'd say, had been outwitted on the rim of the waterhole.

Even so, he'd begun sensing, that August, a dark sharpening of death's presence. He wondered if he still wrestled with his father's death or with the deaths of soldiers he'd counseled. But no, he decided. More was chilling him, more than the war and the summer's losses. He recalled the night creature, the apparition that he'd seen before the war in his Berlin bedroom. He could feel the monstrous clutch of tentacles and teeth.

Something, Leo thought, was wrong, something perilous beyond words.

Fighting in the German army, perhaps inches away from Leo at times, was an Austrian named Adolf Hitler. Born in 1889, in the city of Braunau, Hitler had lived during his teens in flophouses. He'd dropped out of school to daydream of painting pictures but failed to win acceptance at an art academy. His true obsession was German nationalism. Foreigners, he said, were "scum" and "dirt." Pure-blooded Germans were the world's "Master Race."

In 1914, Hitler was living in Munich, Germany. Entering the German army, he'd planned to ride the crest of Deutschland's victory. While Leo served needy Jewish soldiers, Adolf Hitler thirsted for conquest and won the rank of corporal.

Germany's thrust for victory, however, went awry. Britain and the United States joined the opposing Allied powers. Supplies fell off in Germany, and cities were crushed. When the German High Command surrendered to the Allies in 1918, Germany's economy was in ruins. Leo returned home to tell the Berlin Jewish community of Jews on both sides of the war. Hitler wandered into Munich, embittered by defeat. Jews, he claimed, had sabotaged Germany from within. Deutschland had not lost the war; it had fallen victim to *Dolchstoss*, a stab in the back.

Responding to Hitler's spreading anti-Semitism, German Christians began blaming Jews for the economic decline. Jews, said Christian industrialists, must have worked secretly for Deutschland's surrender. What matter that, according to the Rabbi Baeck's sermons, one hundred thou-

sand Jews had served in the German army—one-sixth of all
Jews in Germany—and that twelve thousand had died? A
German Workers' party formed in a Munich beer hall. One
member, Adolf Hitler, scoffed at Leo Baeck's "sentimental
slop." Jewish businessmen, said Hitler, plotted to consume
the world.

In their Berlin apartment, Leo, Natalie, and Ruth listened
to radio broadcasts carrying Hitler's hysteria. Newspapers
and journals describing the rise in anti-Semitism covered
Leo's desk. Over a hundred Jewish cemeteries had been
vandalized. Jews were fired from jobs and refused service
in stores with meager supplies. Three Jewish university students had been attacked. The radical voice of Adolf Hitler
was promising extreme measures to solve Germany's "Jewish problem."

With welfare funds, Leo arranged for a network of families in Vienna to house temporarily one thousand German
Jewish children of poverty-stricken parents. The children
would be properly clothed and fed. A sense of urgency kept
Leo in constant touch with officers of the Berlin Jewish
community. Steps must be taken, he said, to offset the Jew-
hating. Jews were losing ground in Germany. What they'd
built with such pride was rapidly dissolving.

Natalie Baeck watched the intensity of Leo's efforts. He'd
come home to her from the war preoccupied. Physically, he
was still slim and agile. In his mid-forties, he walked faster
than almost anyone and, seated in a chair, he'd wrap his
arms around the back as if to keep from leaping to another
task. "Could you pause for a breath or two?" Natalie might
say. But knowing that Leo would not stop, she made certain to bring him hot sandwiches and soup.

The communities of Jews in Germany were referring to
Leo as Chief Rabbi of Berlin. He helped raise funds for Jewish war veterans; he joined the Central-Verein, an association of Germans of the Jewish faith; he was elected president of the Allgemeiner Rabbinerverbandes, a group of

Liberal and Orthodox rabbis. He also presided over the Zentralwohlfahrtsstelle, an organization combining German Jewish welfare agencies, and over B'nai B'rith of Germany, a Jewish fraternal order of thirteen thousand members. At the Hochschule, he continued his teaching, raising a few eyebrows with his penchant for new ideas. Females, traditionally excluded from serious study, were invited by Leo to enroll in the seminary. Several young women had read *The Essence of Judaism* and expressly signed up for the Rabbi Baeck's classes.

Arranging student scholarships or writing recommendation letters for teachers in his apartment at Burggrafenstrasse 19, Leo had been counseling Jews between eleven and noon on weekdays. His receiving hours, along with those of other Berlin rabbis, were printed in the Jewish newspaper. Also printed in the daily paper were an increasing number of stories on anti-Semitism. Leo read of Hitler's regrouping the German Workers' party into the National Socialist German Workers' party, the Nazi party. Uniformed squads of SA, or storm troopers, guarded Hitler's meetings and broke up rival groups. Under the symbol of a swastika, the ancient hooked cross, Nazis made plans to create a new Germany by "cleansing" it of Jews.

Hitler had been jailed for trying to overthrow the ruling government, but he was becoming a national hero. Germany, he ranted, must be "a people of the same blood." If the Nazi party won government elections, Germany would have a "rich economy and a gloriously rebuilt army." Nazis would deny land to Jews, throw them out of public office, cast them from German borders. *"Jude verrecke!"*—"Jew perish!"—Hitler proclaimed.

Leo spoke in rebuttal from the *bimahs* of Berlin synagogues, telling congregants to remind Germany of Jewish contributions. Medicine, literature, art, science, philosophy, theology—all held Jewish creations or discoveries. Awakening now an hour before dawn, Leo used the extra time

Leo and Natalie Baeck on an outing, 1930

for his sermons and *Shabbos* messages. His punctuality helped him to carry responsibilities. He was never a moment late to his Hochschule classes. Once, when he called a B'nai B'rith meeting for 7:00 A.M. and no one came by 7:05, he put his books in a valise and quietly left the building.

In 1929, just after Germany began recovering strength, a worldwide depression hit with full force. Millions of people were unemployed. Hitler's words resounded above the panic. "Listen to me!" he cried. "Follow me! Germany shall be miraculously healed." In the 1930 Reichstag elections, Nazis garnered 6.5 million votes. They hadn't ousted the ruling party—headed by Paul von Hindenburg—but they put 107 deputies in the legislature.

By 1932, votes for the Nazis totaled nearly 14 million. Von Hindenburg prevailed as president, but the Nazi party possessed government power. Hundreds of brown-shirted Nazi officers, displaying swastikas on arm bands, marched the boulevards of Berlin. Rocks were hurled into Jewish shop windows; freshly printed posters read Buy German, Not Jewish.

"A passing insanity," Jewish congregants said to Leo. "We belong to Germany." But on January 30, 1933, Adolf Hitler was appointed German chancellor. A euphoria swept through the nation, matched only by dread among Germany's Jews. How had it happened? Jews asked one another. Jewish establishments and services functioned in every German city. Why would Germany support a fanatic like Hitler?

On the night of January 30, Leo and Natalie stood at a parlor window of their third-floor apartment. Torches burned below in the semidarkness, laughter and drunken jeering punctured the air. Hanging by the neck from an iron streetlamp was a huge stuffed doll labeled *Jude*, German for *Jew*. "The dark," Natalie whispered to Leo, looking sadly at the doll, "falls upon us, doesn't it, when we least believe it?"

Leo's voice was hoarse, his face drawn. "The dark menaces," he answered. "But it can be weathered." Striding across the parlor, he opened the front door and hurried down the stairway to the street. At the curb, breathing in the smoke from the lighted torches, he yanked at the rope encircling the doll's neck, untying the floppy figure from its makeshift gallows. Limply the doll lurched forward, lying lifelessly in his arms. Struck by its presence, he freed one of his hands from underneath the cloth body, touching the broad, misshapen head.

Gently, then, like a scribe bent over the calligraphy of an ancient psalm, Leo traced the shapes of the four letters— *J-u-d-e*—that had been scrawled, on Hitler's night, in fresh blood over the doll's chest.

5

To Act With an Unfailing Courage

Wildflowers bloomed in the German countryside. Lavender and yellow fringed the Havel lakes outside the city of Berlin. Spring had arrived—April 1, 1933—yet winds hinted of *sommerfrische*, summer vacation. Leaving the Hochschule, Leo did not wear his overcoat. Usually, at this time, he and Natalie would have been planning their vacation. In past years, they'd visited Italy and Switzerland, toured towns across southern Germany. In the summers of 1925 and 1930, Leo traveled by tramp steamer to the United States. He had revised *The Essence of Judaism* and found it standard reading in American Jewish seminaries.

This April day, however, he could not consider travel. All morning, he'd attended emergency meetings at offices of the Berlin Jewish Community, at the rabbinical association, in a lecture room at the Hochschule. Adolf Hitler had declared a one-day boycott of Jewish stores. Windows in Jewish districts were soap-smeared with the same four letters, *J-u-d-e,*

Max Westfield's portrait of Baeck. It was destroyed on *Kristallnacht*, Night of Crystal Glass, in November 1938.

that had marked the hanging doll. Offices of Jewish doctors and lawyers were also defaced.

Leo had asked his family to stay indoors. Ruth, married now to an accountant named Hermann Berlak, was settled in Berlin. The night before, on *Shabbos*, the family had gone together to services. At the Fasanenstrasse Synagogue, where Leo was preaching, an overflow of people pushed onto the steps and down the aisles. In fear of Boycott Day, Jews had been flocking to their synagogues. Many came who, in past years, had forsaken Judaism for a Christianized culture. "In truth," Leo said to the congregants about the next day's boycott, "it is justice that will be boycotted." He advised Jews to maintain their self-respect and to pray that Hitler would be able to "respect the convictions of others."

At the close of services, the congregation had stood to recite the *Shema*. Swaying to the rhythm of the Hebrew— *"Shema Yisrael Adonai Elohenu Adonai Echad"*—they reaffirmed their testament to God. Voices rang with such fervor that the organist, tears streaming down his face, had stopped playing in accompaniment.

Walking from the Hochschule, Leo could still hear the *Shema* in his ears. Obstructing his vision, however, was a battery of Nazi storm troopers goose-stepping down the street. Before dawn, he'd watched Hitler's secret police, the Gestapo, pasting crude drawings of Jews onto trucks. Hitler's venom, he thought, was ceaseless. In A.D. 324, when Christianity had become the legal religion of the Roman Empire, Jews were urged to renounce their faith and convert. Yet Hitler did not want Jews to be Christians—or Nazis—or even citizens of Germany. He wanted Jews to disappear.

Judenrein, free of Jews, was the latest Nazi password. Leo had repeated it at his morning meetings. "I believe," he'd said at the rabbinical association, "that Hitler intends the end of German Jewry." Grimly, the Liberal and Orthodox rabbis had stayed quiet. Only a few protested, insisting that Germany would come to its senses. Most of the men, less confident than when Leo was a young rabbi from Oppeln, defending Zionism's right to exist, did not oppose him. Wasn't the Rabbi Baeck an international author and a *tsadik*—both scholarly and holy?

Beneath a blue awning on Artilleriestrasse, Leo stopped at a Jewish poultry shop. Stationed outside was a uniformed storm trooper. Gesturing toward a window sign, the trooper hooked the thumb of his other hand over the top of his belt. "Do not buy from Jews!" he read aloud from the sign.

Leo recognized the man as one of the guards dispatched by Hitler to monitor meetings of the Berlin Jewish Community for anti-German ideas. *"Ach!"* the trooper continued. "Isn't it fortunate, Herr Doktor Baeck, that you—whose only customers are Jews—cannot lose business on Boycott Day?"

"Please step aside," Leo answered. "I must visit this shopkeeper."

Laughing, the trooper brushed at the swastika arm band at his left elbow. In an exaggerated gesture, he opened the door, yanking out the aproned shopkeeper waiting inside. "You won't want to smell the unbought chickens," said the trooper, "that will rot without Christians to help them off the shelves."

Purchasing two of the chickens himself—a forbidden action of commerce on *Shabbos* that, this once, he allowed himself—Leo pressed some money into the shopkeeper's apron pocket, encouraging him to be calm. Several moments later, he set off for other Jewish stores—tailor shops, furriers, grocers—visiting them through the afternoon. Ugly slogans were painted everywhere. "We're like lepers," a store owner told Leo, showing him the day's newspapers. Not one editorial had criticized the boycott; no court official or university professor had expressed disapproval of Hitler's treatment of Jews.

By sundown, having left the chickens he'd bought at a Jewish agency, Leo returned home for dinner with Natalie. Both *Shabbos* and Boycott Day had ended. Natalie pleaded with him to rest, but no sooner did she set the table than the parlor filled with Hochschule students. A message, the

Baeck is pictured in the first row, far right, in this 1930s photograph of Hochschule scholars. Most of the students and instructors shown here later lost their lives in the Holocaust.

students said, had been delivered. In the town of Tiengen, on the upper Rhine, troopers had set up a firing range. Vile caricatures of Jewish residents were being used as targets. Christian townspeople, summoned by the troopers, had been issued rifles with an invitation to shoot.

"Where do Jews turn, Herr Doktor Baeck?" the students asked. "Hitler is driving Germany into madness. What shall we do? What can you advise us?"

In the hallway mirror, Leo caught a sideways glimpse of his own reflection. His hair had been graying, and he wore eyeglasses. Yet he rarely thought of himself as aging; his energy remained high. Already, he had considered actions that might be taken for the Jews. He'd made a list, in the past week, of possibilities. He had spoken to Zionists and non-Zionists, to Orthodox scholars and freethinking Liberals. He would write an official letter to Adolf Hitler, requesting negotiations, presenting a reasoned but firm objection to the persecution of Germany's Jews.

In the thick, brass-edged mirror, he suddenly imagined the bearded face of his father, the tall forehead, the piercing eyes. What, he wondered, would the Rabbi Bäck have said to Jewish shopkeepers and students on Boycott Day? How would he have confronted Adolf Hitler? Was his father's spirit and wisdom somewhere nearby?

Turning back toward the students who awaited him, Leo was certain only that Samuel Bäck would have expected the son who'd become a rabbi, who'd followed in the footsteps of earliest Judaic teaching, to act with an unfailing courage.

Since April, Jewish children had been pelted with stones. Teenagers recruited by Hitler would corner young Jews on the streets. Leo had a granddaughter of his own, Marianne, born to Ruth and Hermann Berlak. Janne, he'd nicknamed her, his "special joy." Once, as he walked with Janne in a park, they'd come upon a little girl sobbing under a tree. The child was covered with mud and the manure of horses. "They've ruined my dress," she wept. "They called me a dirty Jew."

The help asked of Leo by the Hochschule students on Boycott Day was asked by Jews across Germany. Community leaders in Essen, a western city, suggested that Leo form a national organization of German Jews. "You'll represent us to the Nazis," said the men. "No one else will be considered for the post. Your name means something to every Jew in Germany."

By September of 1933, on Rosh Hashanah, the Reichsvertretung, or Representative Council of Jews in Germany, opened its doors. Leo Baeck was its president; offices were located on Kantstrasse 158, midway between the Baeck apartment and the Hochschule. Leo would disperse funds received from Germany's Jews and from abroad. Welfare and educational programs would be supervised. Aid would be given to Jews who wanted to emigrate from Germany.

Somehow, Leo managed to attend all the meetings of or-

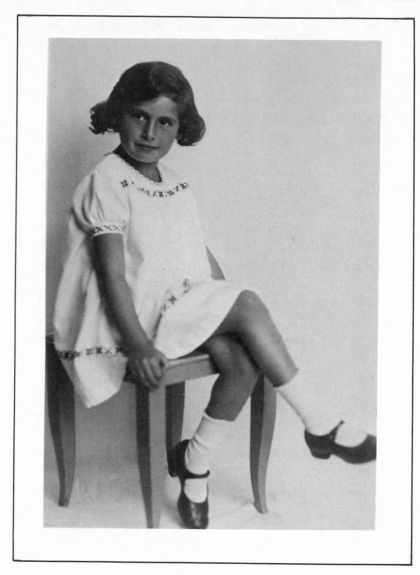

Baeck's only grandchild, Marianne "Janne" Berlak, on whom
he doted

ganizations he headed. His letter to Adolf Hitler was written at the Reichsvertretung and sent to the entire German
cabinet. The letter, the only one ever written officially to
Hitler by a Jew, emphasized attacks on Jewish students and

the recent government edict against Jews practicing law or entering, or remaining, in civil service. Physical and economic abuse against Jews, said the letter, would sever their ability to benefit the fatherland. No country could condone such treatment if it wanted to "maintain honor and decency."

Leo's letter was never answered. Because of his reputation, however, and because Hitler was wary of world opinion, Leo was not harassed for sending it. From the Reichsvertretung offices, he issued a formal statement to Germany's half-million Jews. Freedom, he said, was not based on a "wheel of happenings" but existed independently from whatever pulled it "in another direction." Still, he added, Jews must face certain facts. Though the first German Jewish settlement was over a thousand years old, Hitler was pushing Jews to leave Germany, refusing to see them as human beings of worth. Hitler invented for his convenience an inferior Jew who didn't exist. "It was Adolf Hitler," Leo said, "who predicted that only propaganda was needed to sell his brand of anti-Semitism, that no end of 'stupid people' would buy it."

By 1934, thirty-five thousand Jews, including large numbers of rabbis, had emigrated from Germany. Leo himself was offered a teaching post at Oxford University in England. Declining, he told his co-workers that he must stay in Germany. Juggling his hours at the Reichsvertretung with his other community duties, his Hochschule classes, and his services at synagogues, he visited secular schools in Berlin. Jewish children were frequently spit on, hit, and made the brunt of verbal cruelties. Teachers forced them to sing anti-Jewish songs. "When Jewish blood spurts from the knife," a little boy was whipped into singing, "then everything will be fine."

"Our children," Leo reported to his Reichsvertretung staff, "need to be removed from public schools. We will open more Jewish classrooms."

One *Shabbos*, a group of girls and boys gathered around

Leo in the Prinzregentenstrasse Synagogue. "Why does Germany hate us?" they asked. "Why do people wish us to suffer?"

Leo had been asked similar questions by Janne on their walks in the park. "We hope," he answered the children, "that those who hate so unfairly will find their way back to God. But, remember, you will always be supported by Him, by the One. You must never lose faith."

From 1934 to 1935, the Nazis enacted nineteen laws against Jews. Additional edicts in 1935, called the Nuremberg Laws, left Germany's Jews shocked. Their citizenship was revoked; they could be arrested by the Gestapo at will and imprisoned without cause in detention camps or jails. Marriage between Jew and non-Jew was a criminal offense. Public beaches, resorts, universities, and phones were off-limits, as were non-Jewish hospitals, barbershops, and railroad dining cars and sleepers. Specific shopping hours for Jews were designated. Jewish automobiles would be assigned separate "Jew numbers."

When the Nuremberg Laws were announced, Leo was composing a sermon for Yom Kippur. Nazis controlled radio broadcasts, and from a radio on his desk he heard the description of each new law. Hitler, said the broadcast, had assumed the titles of führer—or leader—supreme head of state and commander in chief of the armed forces. He'd ordered mass book burnings of thousands of undesirable books, including Herr Doktor Leo Baeck's *The Essence of Judaism*. Books were driven from libraries to bonfires in public squares.

At that moment, Hitler's voice broke through radio static. In the future, Hitler boasted, German infants would be born of Aryan parents: white-skinned people of non-Jewish descent. Infants born of other circumstances would not be considered German. True children of the Third Reich, the third state in Germany's history, would be taught "the ultimate realization of the necessity of blood purity."

An impassioned Baeck addresses the Reichsvertretung, 1934.

While static buzzed at him, Leo stopped writing his sermon. Angrily, he crumpled the pages on his desk into a basket. Then, with an echo of the Nuremberg Laws in the room, he put a clean paper sheet in front of him. His eyeglasses had slipped down the bridge of his nose, but, determined, he pushed them back in place. He would write another sermon, he told himself, one that would address the catastrophe, the essence of Nazi Germany. Until this day, he'd been careful not to irritate the Nazis into closing the Reichsvertretung, a risk that now seemed necessary. Oh, my Germany, Leo thought in a moment's nostalgia. The pinewoods, the splendid cities, the palaces, churches, and synagogues, the art, music, and books—everything that was, for Jews, to disappear . . .

In his childhood, he'd learned from his father the valiant yet often tortured story of his people. He carried that story within him; he carried, also, *das Gebot*, the Commandment of God. Caution would not temper the sermon he must give on Yom Kippur. He would pay, he knew, for what he was about to write. But for his father, Samuel, and for his mother, Eva; for his sisters and brothers; for Natalie, Ruth, Hermann, and Janne; for every Jew who'd ever trembled from persecution, and for every Jew who cherished freedom, he put his pen to the waiting page.

6

At Any Risk

A jagged crack slashed the prison wall from ceiling to floor. On a cot, Leo sat among stains and residues of spilled food. Since his arrest the day before, he had been transferred from Prinz-Albrecht-Strasse jail to a basement cell at a Berlin air base. He was not allowed to call Natalie. Two Gestapo officers had taken him from the synagogue in a locked wagon. "You'll come with us, Herr Doktor Baeck," they'd said. "Why did you not show us your sermon?"

He had never intended, of course, for the Nazis to review his speech. One of the copies he'd delivered to other rabbis in Berlin turned up at the Interior Ministry for clearance. *"Verboten!"*—"Forbidden!"—was the verdict. No synagogue, the Nazis ordered, could permit the reading of such trash. Offenders would be punished.

The sun haloed the lectern at the Fasanenstrasse Synagogue on the morning of Yom Kippur. Gestapo officers flanked the entryway. From the *bimah*, Leo had addressed his words to the solemn congregants. "We stand before our God," he'd read from his soon-to-be-famous sermon. "With that same force with which we have confessed our sins, personal and collective, let us say that the lies uttered against us, the false charges made against our faith and its defenders are hateful. Let us trample these falsehoods beneath our feet. . . .

"We are filled with sorrow and pain," he'd told the many hundreds of Jews. "We stand before our God . . . we bow to Him, [but] we stand upright and erect before man."

The Gestapo arrested him beneath the Holy Ark. He'd laid the Torah in its white covering, closed the Ark, and removed his *tallis* before following the glint of gun barrels. In jail, his papers and wristwatch were taken from him, yet he'd refused to react. He ate nothing. He would not loosen his tie or unbutton his vest. All night, he sat rigidly on the cot, watching the dark wall with its crack slowly lighten with day. Now, hearing a guard rattling the cell door, he barely shifted his head.

"You've had luck, rabbi Jew," the guard said. "A temporary reprieve. Some swine correspondent for the London *Times* discovered your arrest. Let foreign papers see how well we treat scum. You are released. We'll deal with you later."

Thrust out on a runway of the air base, Leo was surrounded by non-German newspapermen. Protests over his arrest, he was told, had been sent to Germany by wire; objections from foreign agencies must have persuaded the Nazis not to harm their important prisoner. Had he been mistreated? Leo was asked. The mistreatment, he replied, was of all the German Jews.

A week following the arrest, a written condemnation was delivered to German embassies in the United States. Twelve prominent ministers, among them Reinhold Niebuhr and Harry Emerson Fosdick, censured the harassment of the Rabbi Leo Baeck. His imprisonment, wrote the clergymen, was "unbelievable to us." His Yom Kippur sermon was being distributed to international journals.

The Fasanenstrasse Synagogue, where Baeck was arrested
by the Gestapo beneath the Holy Ark

Home with Natalie, Leo tried to lessen her worries for him.
The reality of the situation, however, was that anti-Semitism was everywhere. The salute *"Heil* Hitler!" thundered
across Germany. Nazi propaganda chief, Joseph Goebbels,
a tiny man with a childhood limp, banned all democratic lit-

erature in Deutschland. And Nazi henchman, Hermann
Goering, was awarded control of the Gestapo and the reg-
ular police. "It is not justice that I have to carry out," Goering crowed from speakers' platforms. "It is elimination."

Emigrating had become the only safety for Germany's Jews.
Yet even Hitler's fanatic Jew-hating did not prompt other
countries to raise refugee quotas. Foreign diplomats and
presidents turned deaf ears toward the pleas of German
Jewish communities. Jews might leave the Reich, but how
many of them would find residence elsewhere?

Arguing at consulate and state department offices, Leo
secured as many visas as possible to France, England, Palestine, the United States, South America, or South Africa.
He'd begun encouraging young Jews to leave Germany.
Youth, he said, deserved a place "to breathe in the light,"
to be "protected from disagreeable and evil things." He
comforted one young man who, by going to the United
States, would abandon an elderly father. "You must forge
the way," Leo said. "Next year, your father may be granted
a visa to join you."

"But shouldn't I stay to care for him?" the young man
asked. "What if the Nazis lose power? Wouldn't I have left
without reason?"

Leo had learned to counter the arguments of the bewil-
dered and fearful. Bravery was needed to leave one's home
and family, to cross oceans and continents, to build a new
life in an alien place. "Your father," Leo answered, "will
know you've made another home for him. If the Nazis
weaken, you can return to Germany."

The final question blurted out by the young man was familiar to Leo. "And you, Herr Doktor Baeck? Aren't *you*
leaving? Surely a man of your stature easily obtains a visa?"

"I will remain in Germany," Leo said, "to watch out for
those who haven't yet gone."

Stories of persecution kept increasing, and Leo wrote his
own scattered family members about emigrating. Several
nieces and nephews sought his counsel in Berlin. Jews of

Frankfurt and Düsseldorf were being dragged into church-
yards and gouged with knives in swastika patterns. Neither
police nor passersby answered screams for help. In the Baeck
parlor, Natalie would wring her hands in despair. "In Berlin," she'd say, "Gestapo spies dress as civilians. They wait
to arrest Leo again. Eight neighbors were murdered in the
night. Frau Golden, the seamstress, was strangled with her
bedclothes."

"Let me send you to England," Leo would urge Natalie.
"Friends will seek residence for you, and for Ruth, Hermann, and Janne. I'll come when my work is finished."

But Natalie would not leave her husband. Nor would Ruth
agree to go. By August of 1936, Natalie was thin and star-
tlingly pale. Her hands shook, and she jumped at any sound.
When visiting, Ruth would find her mother staring into
space. Leo continued to speak of England but, in a compro-
mise, took Natalie on vacation to Switzerland. Natalie would
rest, he told Ruth. She would not have to worry about the
Gestapo killing Jews in the night. And in letters home to
Berlin, he described her cure. She was hiking with him along
trails under a radiant sun. She was "recovering slowly with
good food and air."

The trip to Switzerland colored Natalie's cheeks through
the month of October. She assured Leo that she was fine,
and for a while he believed her. By November, however,
the strain had reappeared. Awakening at night without her
beside him, Leo would throw off his covers, leap to the floor,
and call her name. Sometimes, she stood at a window, lis-
tening for the goose-step of Nazi boots. How could he help
her? he'd ask himself, sensing once more the clutch of tentacles. Natalie had never deserved a moment's suffering. She
had given unending love.

On March 2, 1937, Natalie Baeck took to her bed. A Jewish doctor was summoned but could not pinpoint a specific
illness. "The illness," Leo said tightly from his wife's side,
"is Nazi Germany."

All that March day, though she touched Leo's forehead

Natalie Baeck died in 1937 at the age of fifty-eight.

when he bent over her, Natalie seemed too tired to speak. Ruth, Hermann, and Janne gathered in the bedroom but could barely rouse her. Two days passed by without improvement. Then, on the third morning, Natalie could not be awakened at all. Grief-stricken, Leo summoned the doctor. His wife, stated the certificate left on the bedroom bureau, was dead at the age of fifty-eight from a cerebral hemorrhage.

"My sympathies, Herr Doktor Baeck," murmured the doctor. "Yet I depart now. The Nazis threaten to shoot me for practicing medicine."

Just as he had said *Kaddish* at his father's gravesite, Leo offered the prayer at Natalie's grave. Her coffin was lowered into the ground at Weissensee, Berlin's Jewish cemetery. From Proverbs 31:29, Leo made his tribute: "Many a woman shows how capable she is; but you excel them all." He had chosen the last five words for her gravestone: "But you excel them all."

Natalie Baeck had died a victim of inhumanity. In his final words over her grave, Leo said: "You who were so pure, so honest, so clear; you who were so bright, so true, so pious, so devout, so good, so helpful, so warm. . . . You have gone home and left us without you."

Faced with the destruction of German Jewry, Leo had struggled for resolutions. Now, with Natalie dead, his struggles would find no rest. Unflinchingly, his Yom Kippur sermon resounding throughout Europe, he would put himself further in harm's way. What, he'd question, should stop him? What else, with Natalie gone, must counter tragedy but God's mandate to act?

7

"The Synagogues Are Burning!"

Thirty-two nations had met in Evian-les-Bains, France, to solve the plight of Germany's Jews. Suggested by U.S. President Franklin Delano Roosevelt, the 1938 conference was meant to raise Jewish settlement quotas. Hitler had recently annexed Austria. Before the conference, the führer ordered mass arrests of Jews in Nuremberg, Munich, and Dortmund. Jewish valuables were seized there by the SS, special, black-shirted Nazi guards.

Yet in the nine days of the Evian conference, the thirty-two nations offered no extra aid. The representatives knew of Nazi beatings, robberies, and murders of Jews. They knew that international money collected for Jewish welfare was frequently stolen by the Gestapo. Still, each of the nations, concerned with unemployment or politics at home, retreated from accepting more German Jews.

As the conference ended, Leo was commanded to appear on a Saturday at Gestapo headquarters. He would be drilled about subversive activities at the Reichsvertretung and at the

Hochschule. He flatly refused to go. "It is the Sabbath," he said to police in the hallway of his apartment. "I don't deal with Nazis on the Sabbath."

Again, his reputation saved him from severe punishment or death. At sundown on that *Shabbos*, he traveled south with three Jews to a faraway spot at the German-Swiss border. A car had been provided by a merchant from Hamburg. The outing, planned by Leo as a border crossing, was to look like a traveling wedding party: prospective bride and groom, rabbi, and family friend.

Some Jews without visas tried crawling across the German border into Switzerland. If they were caught, they were shot. The young man and woman of Leo's wedding party were actually a brother and sister denied visas by a spiteful Nazi official. The sister was dying of a heart ailment and yearned to spend her last months on non-Nazi soil. Borrowing the car, Leo had advised sister and brother to pose as an engaged couple. He brought along a co-worker from the Reichsvertretung to serve as driver and friend.

The area chosen for crossing was a small, sparsely patrolled lake where the brother, an expert swimmer, could pull his sister through the water. On route, the car had been stopped twice by Gestapo officers. Leo presented himself as the rabbi performing the wedding, and the driver was flagged onward. A few hours before dawn, the car was steered off the road and parked in a grove of trees at the lake. Brother and sister profusely thanked Leo and his companion; trembling, they began removing their outer clothing. Pants, shirts, and a skirt were bundled into a bag.

The left door of the car inched open as the couple prepared to crawl down a swampy stretch of ground beneath eye level of any roaming patrols. "What if my water weight drowns us both?" the young woman asked Leo in a spasm of doubt. "What if you, Herr Doktor Baeck, are arrested on your ride back to Berlin?"

A rustling in some marsh leaves was only a small animal disturbed from its sleep. "You and your brother," Leo said, "will swim to freedom on Switzerland's shore. As for our ride to Berlin, it will, I promise you, be uneventful."

Two weeks afterward, having arranged dozens of such border crossings, Leo received word from members of the B'nai B'rith that sister and brother were safely ensconced in a Swiss farmhouse. The farm owners were a man and wife Leo had met when he'd taken Natalie on vacation.

Illegal crossings persuaded the Nazis to erect barbed wire along miles of German borders. Hitler wanted total control of Jewish evacuation. When the Evian nations would not provide higher refugee quotas, he ordered the incarceration of thousands of Jews into concentration camps. Men, women, and children were arrested, torn from their families, and herded into freight cars running on special tracks to the camps. Catholics, gypsies, and the elderly were also on Hitler's list. Over fifty prison camps operated in Germany; the harsher ones were Buchenwald, near Weimar; Dachau, near Munich; Ravensbrück, near Mecklenburg; and Sachsenhausen, near Berlin.

Just eight months after Natalie Baeck's death, Hitler was using his powers to plan an attack against Jews living outside the camps. On November 9, 1938, *Kristallnacht*, or Night of Crystal Glass, would reverberate through Germany. "At least," Leo later told Ruth, "Natalie is at peace." At least she did not suffer this "latest great blasphemy."

On November 7, a young Jew avenged his father's deportation into Poland by shooting an official of the German embassy in Paris. Immediately, Hitler seized upon the incident. Over the next two days, police, storm troopers, Gestapo, and SS squads were armed with incendiary bombs and rifles. Christian citizens were issued hammers, torches, and axes to help "dismantle" Jewish property.

Leo was alone in his apartment on the night of November 9. The first tremors of bombs and shattered glass had tilted his menorah, a holiday candle holder, onto its side. Crowds were suddenly in the streets, and he'd thrown open his

Jewish prisoners en route to Baden-Baden at the onset of the Holocaust

Berlin Jews are herded to Sachsenhausen concentration camp.

windows. "The synagogues are burning!" someone shouted at him. "The synagogues!"

He grabbed his suit jacket and, for the first time in his adult life, went into public without wearing vest or tie. Running across boulevards, squares, alleyways, and parks, he wove through mobs wielding their axes, plunging past debris littering the streets. No matter how deeply he'd been troubled by the opulence of German synagogues, he could not believe what was happening. The sanctity of temples built to God, to Judaism's heritage, was being brutally defiled. Axes had smashed synagogue windows and chopped seats into wooden chunks. Torches were charring Holy Arks and burning the parchment pages of Torah.

On one boulevard, prayer books lay ripped in an ashy heap. A burning mattress, thrown by Nazis from inside an apartment, sent thick fumes into the November air. For a moment, Leo leaned against a streetlamp on Oranienburgerstrasse, his chest heaving. To his right, beneath an awning, a black-coated man stooped over a thin, oddly bent boy. Looking up, the man recognized Leo and identified himself as a doctor. The boy, he said, was a Jew dropped by the Gestapo from a third-story window. Both arms and legs were broken.

"May I help you move him to a hospital?" Leo asked. But a private car, with stretcher, had already been ordered. The doctor explained that he, in fact, was a Christian. Eyes moist, he apologized to Leo for the terrible ravishment of the Jews, for the horror of the flames and the devastating ruin.

Not all Christians in Germany were anti-Semitic. The "little people, the good people," Leo called those who offered help. Yet Christians bearing hatred would destroy, on *Kristallnacht*, more than two hundred synagogues and eight thousand Jewish stores. Oppeln's synagogue would burn, its tower streaking the night with fiery veins. Gone would be the *bimah* where Leo welcomed his first congregants and saw the pretty, brown-eyed Natalie Hamburger. In Berlin, the Fasanenstrasse Synagogue would become an empty shell.

The synagogue in Oppeln, where Leo Baeck first served as a rabbi, was set aflame *(below)* by Nazi mobs on *Kristallnacht.*

Its 1912 cornerstone, marking the year when even the German kaiser and army guards attended opening services, was crushed. As the synagogue itself collapsed, fire engines stood nearby, driverless and unused.

Almost one thousand German Jews would die on the Night of Crystal Glass. Leo's final stop before returning to his apartment was a hospital for Jewish children. Aghast, he saw the broken windows, the torn and dirtied bedding tossed into the street. Huddled outside were ill and shivering girls and boys, nightgowns stiffened by cold. The Gestapo came, they told him. All the children had been forced from bed and made to walk in bare feet over the shattered glass. Some had been rescued by parents. Others, orphans like themselves, were fending alone.

Leo counted sixteen homeless and helpless children. They must, he said, come with him. They would sleep on blankets or beds in the Rabbi Baeck's apartment until he found them safe quarters and doctors to examine them. Though German Jewish doctors had lost their licenses, they still tended to Jewish patients.

One little boy, looking tubercular, was too sick to walk. Hoisting the child in his arms, Leo organized the fifteen remaining children into a double line. Slowly, walking in front, he directed his charges through a maze of Berlin streets, ignoring the clusters of hammer-wielding men and women. The children kept saying his name as if to console themselves that such an important rabbi would care for them. And like the pied piper, Leo led them, barefoot, bleeding, and half-frozen as they were, aside flaming stores and synagogues, to the warmth of his own rooms.

Hope for a lessening of Nazi malice ended on the night of November 9, 1938. The German government and the populace had conspired together to hurt the Jews. On the next *Shabbos*, honored by German Jews in warehouses, concentration camps, schoolrooms, and crippled synagogues, Leo said of *Kristallnacht*, "One thing, we thought, would bind

More than two hundred synagogues, including this one in Frankfurt, were destroyed on *Kristallnacht*.

The Fasanenstrasse Synagogue, site of Baeck's arrest, in ruins

. . . [Christians and Jews] together: a reverence for that place to which men come in order that they be made one with the Eternal, raised above the narrowness and hardship of their everyday life, where the invisible is made known to them and the infinite silence embraces them."

That place—church, synagogue, shrine, mosque—had not been kept inviolate for Jews by Hitler and his henchmen. Gestapo chief Hermann Goering, jubilant over the burning of the German synagogues, answered Leo Baeck's latest sermon. "I have no personal conscience," said Goering. "Adolf Hitler is my only conscience."

8

An Unparalleled Burden

In history, Jews were not the sole victims of persecution. Differences in ideas, aims, or beliefs had, over the centuries, triggered small battles and large wars among men. From the Stone Age onward, human beings killed for possessions, suffered cruelties at the hands of others. Yet Jews bore an unparalleled burden. The government of a modern, civilized country terrorized Jews just because they were Jews. Hitler's fantasies of a Master Race demanded the mass exile of the Hebrew people.

In the wake of *Kristallnacht*, Nazis seized Jewish businesses, murdered dozens of Jewish school children, and dumped trainloads of Jews into camps or fields in Poland or Czechoslovakia. By 1939, two-thirds of Germany's Jews had voluntarily fled the Reich. Some went to England when, after the Night of Crystal Glass, refugee quotas were grudgingly raised. Others escaped to wherever they could. Visas, suddenly black-marketed, were often stolen by police, then resold to owners at exorbitant fees. Rumors flew like wild birds in Germany: Argentina might raise its quotas; Bolivia was now lenient. With the Nazi stranglehold tightening, Germany's Jews were frantic.

One September morning in 1939, Leo's key would not open the doors to the Reichsvertretung. Nazis had changed the locks. Two weeks earlier, Hitler's armies had attacked Poland. In short order, Denmark, Norway, Holland, and Belgium would fall to the Reich. Descending from the Hitlerian dream, World War II would begin—a war Hitler intended, this time, to win.

Shut out of the Reichsvertretung, Leo invited his coworkers to meet in his apartment. He spoke of his years in World War I, of prayers over gangrenous limbs and gaping wounds, of sermons at gravesites. Why should any Jew, he asked, be surprised at new violence? Only Jews seemed, at last, to fathom the führer's savagery. Even the German Catholic church, awed by Hitler's wrath against it, had honored his birthday by imploring God's favors upon him.

At his apartment door, Leo had found two letters delivered from a secret mail drop in Portugal. Ordinary mail was opened by the Nazis, and phones were tapped. One letter came from a Jewish child in England. During nights over the past summer, Leo had managed to fill an empty train with Jewish children and a Jewish engineer, chaperoning them on a risky escape to London. On the dusty floor of the train, he'd kneeled among terrified boys and girls. "Your mothers and fathers," he'd said, "want you to be safe. Germany is not safe. Friends in England will provide homes until your parents reach you."

Many of the parents, Leo knew, would never survive Nazi Germany. They might be evacuated to a camp, whipped or beaten, casually killed. They could starve in Poland or Czechoslovakia, lose access to England. But the children on the train would live. "The sun shall not smite thee by day," he quoted from Psalm 121 to the boys and girls, "nor the moon by night."

After the children were settled in England, Leo returned to Berlin. A former German rabbi begged him to remain in London, but he'd waved off the idea. "You are sixty-six years old, Herr Doktor," the other rabbi countered. "Everyone predicts a bloodbath from Hitler. Things will be worse for Jews. How long can you stay in Germany?"

"Until the last Jew," Leo replied, "is saved."

His interest was hardly stirred, therefore, by the second mail-drop letter. From the United States, the organizations of Central Conference of American Rabbis and Independent Order of B'nai B'rith offered rescue—an appointment as associate rabbi at a synagogue in Cincinnati, Ohio. Rabbis could be issued nonquota visas without having to await clearance. Yet Leo folded the letter back into its envelope. Politely, he would write his thanks while explaining that he was "not contemplating" any move from Berlin.

World War II, which eventually united Germany, Italy, and Japan against Great Britain, Russia, France, China, and the United States, would indeed be a bloodbath. German armies left a trail of unburied and brutalized bodies. In Jewish villages, soldiers were particularly vicious. Men, women, and children were lined up and shot until streets were awash with blood. Brutality reigned also in cities of high Jewish learning: Munich, where Albert Einstein, renowned physicist, first became interested in mathematics; Vienna, where Sigmund Freud, founder of psychoanalysis, began exploring the unconscious mind. Jews were kidnapped and forced into hard labor. The Gestapo shot some victims for amusement or stripped them naked in public. Young girls were assaulted; elders had their beards ripped out by hand. Anti-Semitic citizens in Poland and Russia openly attacked Jews.

Leo now insisted that Ruth, Hermann, and Janne leave Germany. "You must go!" he told his daughter. When visas to England were obtained for the Berlaks, he went to supervise the packing. Each fastened suitcase in the vesti-

Leo's daughter, Ruth Berlak, and granddaughter, Janne, in 1938, before they fled Nazi Germany for England

bule gave him satisfaction. He had brought fruit for the journey and chocolate for fourteen-year-old Janne. "A man I'd never seen put the chocolate in my pocket," he said to Janne. "Many people help. There are good Christians hiding Jews in attics. Last week, someone handed me ration stamps for food that's grown scarce in the war, saying, 'You dropped these.' Of course, I hadn't."

Leo traveled as far as Hamburg with Ruth and her family.

He would see them again, he said. He would try, someday, to join them. Yes, he would write letters. Embracing Ruth, he could almost feel Natalie's presence beside him. She would have been so relieved that the Berlaks were going. She might have urged him to flee, but she would have known his answer.

This time, before returning to Berlin, Leo embarked on a solitary mission. Jews were being ordered to surrender the silver kept in their homes. In his dining room, Leo had stored some religious objects that Natalie brought to the marriage. Bequeathed to her by her father, the objects had been collected by her grandfather. The day before bidding the Berlaks good-bye, Leo had polished the silver one last time. At supper, he'd slipped the objects into a pillowcase, vowing that the Gestapo would not have them. He would carry the pillowcase out of Berlin to Hamburg. He would dispose of Natalie's mementos with honor.

Renting a rowboat at a Hamburg wharf, he climbed onto a splintered seat with his cargo. He pulled a small map from his vest pocket and checked a penciled area on the front. When he was finished, he picked up the oar handles that jutted off the sides of the boat and slowly began rowing from shore. Sun dotted his route toward the harbor where the Elbe River brimmed into a channel of the North Sea. Fishermen gaped at him from other boats, baffled by the sight of the distinguished-looking gentleman who nodded at them but did not speak.

The place where Leo stopped rowing was one he had carefully marked with arrows on his map. A tidal flow in the harbor would sweep away loose materials into the sea, unavailable to divers or swimmers. Leo picked up the pillowcase and emptied it onto his lap. He let himself touch the small center candle holder on the menorah, a silent gesture to Natalie. Then, resolute, he gathered up everything in his arms and leaned sideways over the edge of the boat.

The silver menorah and ornamented spice boxes fell from

him into the rippling channel. A lid caught a sparkle of sun-
light before it disappeared. Droplets splashed upward into
Leo's face. He could taste the saltiness of his own tears but,
shaking his head, he sat upright. Steadily, he pulled the oar
handles toward him. A lapping of waves at the prow of the
rowboat did not for a moment distract him.

Rowing back toward the fishing wharf at Hamburg, Leo
felt at peace. In spite of what still might be lost—in spite of
what still, for the Jews, might crumble or disappear—the
Nazis of Germany would never again have any part of his
beloved wife, Natalie.

Without notice, the Reichsvertretung offices were re-
opened. Summoned by the Gestapo, Leo was presented with
ultimatums. The Reichsvertretung, renamed the Reichsvereinigung, would be controlled by Nazis. Leo and his staff
would be retained. They were to go on handling applica-
tions for Jewish visas. "Your people beg to get out," snarled
an officer. "You and your God-babbling will make arrange-
ments. You will keep serving your Jews."

He could, of course, have refused. But what would have
been accomplished? If Jews didn't staff the Reichsvereinigung, Nazis would. Every Jew whom Leo helped to emigrate was one less victim of the camps or of deportation.

Some German Jews were aghast at the conditions of Leo's
reappointment. Was the Rabbi Baeck, they asked, actually
working for Nazis? Had he deserted his people? No, Leo tried
to assure them. He could do more from inside than outside
the Reichsvereinigung. He would assist all Jews to leave
Germany. He would continue welfare for the needy. He
would act as a buffer between the Nazis and the Jews.

Leo's closest co-worker was a man named Otto Hirsch.
Born in Stuttgart, Hirsch was a hardy outdoorsman who had
become a lawyer. He and Leo kept the Reichsvereinigung
office staff active. If news reports were bad, the two men
suggested what steps might be taken. Often, the only prac-
tical action was to reapply for visas and passports.

On the day that news arrived of the *Einsatzgruppen,* Leo talked a French official into issuing twelve visas. *Einsatzgruppen* were the mobile killing units of the SS that had invaded Poland with orders to murder as many civilians as possible, especially Jews. The units traveled in gun-equipped vans that later would enclose victims in fumes of poisonous gas.

Reports also reached the Reichsvereinigung of Jews fleeing Germany by boat. In many cases, such voyages failed. The ship *St. Louis* carried over nine hundred Jews whose U.S. visas were invalidated in transit by presidential decree. Hungry and heartsick, the Jewish passengers were stranded for a month on the Atlantic Ocean before being allowed to sail to France, England, Belgium, and Holland. Other boats were refused entry to any country and had to turn back toward Germany. The *Struma,* a dilapidated cattle boat, sank in the Black Sea with 769 Jews aboard. On escape ships intercepted by Nazis, travelers were shot or bludgeoned to death, stripped of valuables, and tossed overboard.

"We Jews will suffer," Leo acknowledged privately to Otto Hirsch. "Some of us will die. But we will survive."

With Hirsch's contacts in Stuttgart, Leo made connections with an underground movement of Christian industrialists. The half-dozen men, sickened by the killings in Germany, agreed to petition Hitler to leave Jewish workers on their payrolls. The industrialists, daring arrest and ruin, met in Leo's apartment. "So far," they told him, "our petition is not denied. We've lost no Jews and will hire more. So many lives, Herr Doktor Baeck, have been saved by your emigration work, your own underground efforts, your messages to your people. We can certainly shield a thousand Jews from Nazi atrocities."

Hitler was broadcasting his newest wartime tirades from stadiums across Germany. The Reich, he said, would swell magnificently with conquered nations. Any possible means would be used to destroy the remaining millions of "inferior people who increase like vermin."

The Stuttgart underground had developed support to depose Hitler, but most German citizens still idolized the führer. Edicts against Jews received applause. Jews could no longer drive cars, walk on major city streets, appear outside at certain hours, attend public movies, buy new clothes, own typewriters, radios, or other household appliances. They had to purchase yellow cloth and sew on their clothing six-pointed stars—a traditional Jewish symbol called the *Magen David*. Four inches in diameter and imprinted in black with the word *Jude*, stars were to be worn by children as well as adults. "Jews who have completed their sixth year," said the German government, "are forbidden to show themselves in public without the Jew-Star."

By 1941, Nazis closed every Jewish seminary in Germany except the Hochschule. Only three faculty members had not died, been imprisoned in camps, or emigrated. Leo Baeck was one of the three. As misery hovered outside the Hochschule building, he kept teaching his classes. Listeners might include a Gestapo spy, but Leo would outwit him. In retelling the tale of the Jewish family of Maccabees who, in 164 B.C., led Jews to victory in the first war for religious freedom, he was relating a Bible story. He was not inciting the somber-faced Jews in the room to a defense of their faith, was he?

Leo was as committed to celebrating the Jewish holidays as he had been in World War I. The Maccabean victory was honored during Chanukah, the winter festival of lights; spring brought celebration of Purim—marking the downfall of Haman, a fifth-century B.C. Persian tyrant—and of Pesach, or Passover, commemorating the Jews' ancient exodus from Egypt in 1200 B.C. At the Levetzowstrasse Synagogue, the only German synagogue not destroyed on *Kristallnacht*, Leo preached to Jews caught in Berlin. "Each idea remains," he said to the sometimes despairing crowds, not really caring if the Gestapo heard him. "It is permanent. No catastrophe can destroy even one idea."

Nazi laws mandated that all Jews wear yellow stars, like the one shown above.

In September 1941, the last Yom Kippur services graced the *bimah* of the Levetzowstrasse Synagogue. Rolling up the Torah scrolls on the day's final *Ne'ilah* service, Leo watched three Gestapo officers barge down the aisles. The synagogue, announced the Gestapo, would become a deportation center for Jews. The thousands sent to labor camps or to concentration camps would be tabulated in Nazi ledgers at the center. Berlin Jews continuing to celebrate their holidays would have to pray without a synagogue.

Leo and his office co-workers broke the fast of Yom Kippur together. Hannah Karminski and Cora Berliner, who'd worked with Leo at the Reichsvertretung, opened a bottle of wine they'd kept hidden for the dwindling staff. Everyone knew that more Gestapo officers were stationed outside. Using a long-burning candle lit before Yom Kippur to light a new candle at holiday's end, Hannah Karminski repeated words from the *Ne'ilah*. "Open the gate for us," she pronounced softly against the muffled but derisive hoot of Gestapo laughter. "The day is done; the sun is setting, soon to be gone. Let us enter Your gates."

Leo's eyes focused on a tall but empty desk chair in the

Attorney Otto Hirsch was Baeck's closest co-worker at the
Reichsvereiningung. In 1941, he was murdered at the
Mauthausen concentration camp in Austria.

office room. His longtime friend and cohort, Otto Hirsch,
should have been sitting with him to break Yom Kippur fast.
Instead, Hirsch had recently become another casualty of Nazi
crime. He'd been summarily arrested, jailed, and sent to
Mauthausen concentration camp in Austria. No tele-
graphed pleas, even from friends in other countries, secured his release. On June 23, a police officer had come to
Hirsch's apartment. Frau Hirsch was told that her husband
had died of "causes" at Mauthausen. His body was cre-

mated. "The urn," said the officer, "cannot be given over. *Heil* Hitler!"

Each human life, Leo thought as his friend's empty chair faced him, was precious. Each of the Jewish and non-Jewish dead in Hitler's bloodbath, in the death trap of German militarism, was a God-endowed being of soul and body. Sipping the wine, Leo quietly ended his own Yom Kippur fast. Natalie, his father, and Otto Hirsch were gone from him. As long as he lived, he would mourn their deaths. Yet he could tell them now, wherever they were, that hope and love endured. Even as the Gestapo breathed at the door, Leo believed mankind would one day awaken to righteousness. The power of evil, he'd say, had as its only fate to perish.

9

Deportation

Hitler was growing impatient. Cleansing the Reich of Jews was taking too long. And so many other undesirables remained—the old, the frail, and the chronically ill; the political resisters and agitators; the Catholics, the gypsies, the homosexuals, and the unemployed. Even the war had bogged down. German armies were suffering losses on Russian terrain. United States bombers were attacking Berlin.

On July 31, 1941, Hitler authorized a "Final Solution of the Jewish Question." The secret operation enlisted all agencies of the German government. Stage One turned the largest concentration camps, now operating throughout the Reich, into killing centers. Airtight chambers, masquerading as shower stalls or thatched huts, were constructed at the camps to receive fumes or pellets of poisonous gas—carbon monoxide or fast-killing Zyklon-B.

For the first time in world history, murder would be conceived of and conducted on an assembly-line basis. Hitler's orders were exact: *Exterminate the six or seven million Jews left in the Reich. Admit the operation to no unauthorized persons.* Auschwitz, a camp operating in Poland's Upper Silesia, became the main killing center. Easily reached by rail, Auschwitz would house five separate death units, each with a gas chamber and a huge cremating oven. Marched into the "showers," unsuspecting Jews would die by the thousands from the gas. Attendants would pry out gold fillings from dead mouths or shear off locks of hair for stuffing German pillows.

Leo heard stories almost too terrible to believe. He knew nothing of the secret gas chambers at Auschwitz, but other horrors were described to him. Jews were being killed with acid that ate away the flesh. Soiled with their own urine and feces, they were shoveled into mass graves. Jewish babies were ripped from their mothers' arms and severed in half on Nazi bayonets. In Poland, bureaucrats called the concentration camp Sobibor an all-year recreational area for children. "That is not true!" sobbed a grief-stricken woman in Leo's apartment. Her twelve-year-old nephew, starving in the Warsaw ghetto, had been kidnapped from his bed and sent with two hundred other children to Sobibor. The boy's postcard home, reading of "good health" and "happiness," contained a family code. "Death!" the child's aunt cried to Leo. "My nephew wrote *death*! He hurt no one! He has no chance to grow up!"

Sometimes Leo just sat with relatives of the dead. His presence soothed them. Daily, he visited the deportation center in the Levetzowstrasse Synagogue, consoling the departing evacuees. Of Berlin's ninety thousand Jews, twenty-five thousand had, voluntarily or by force, disappeared. With continued evacuation to the camps, thirty-five thousand more would go. *Transports are shipped east to do labor,* stated a government bulletin. Words such as *east, labor,* and *resettlement* were open to question: What was the real destination of resettled Jews?

At first, Leo and his Reichsvereinigung co-workers helped

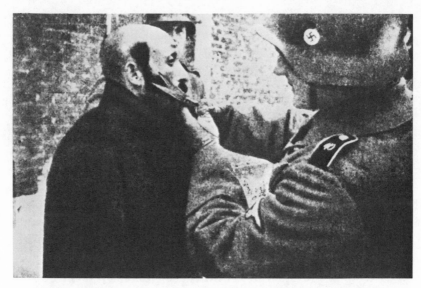

Prior to deportation, a prisoner has his beard shorn by a
Nazi guard.

Jews whose names appeared on the deportation lists to or-
ganize whatever belongings were permitted them. SS officers led each grim pilgrimage of five hundred to the railway
station. Nazi cameramen recorded frightened glances and
gaunt faces. Any Jew causing trouble—even a tearful in-
fant—was immediately shot. Any family member clinging to
a departing loved one was similarly killed.

Leo had hoped to speak to every Jew on the center's lists.
By 1942, however, he stopped his daily visits. More could
be done, he'd found, in back streets and alleys. Young Jews
in hiding arranged through intermediaries to meet him.
Crawling from sewers, chimneys, or eaves, they gasped out
messages for their families. "Can you send a letter abroad,
Herr Doktor Baeck?" they'd ask. "Can you tell my relatives
I'm alive?" Nodding, Leo would, in turn, present a tiny scrap
of paper. "Go here," he'd whisper, having written down a
location where escape by boat, car, or midnight border
crossing might be possible.

Slipping between stairwells or across arcades, Leo narrowly missed the Nazi patrols. He knew he'd soon be arrested, that his name would no longer shield him. Small groups of resisters were living in the German forests. A few assembled makeshift pipe bombs, throwing them into offices and killing Gestapo or SS guards. Yet not only were Nazi casualties small, but fifty to two hundred Jews were hanged in retribution for each murdered officer. "Jews have old eyes," Leo had said. Didn't they watch rather than fight back militarily? Hadn't Torah taught them that vengeance belonged to God, not to man? And, Leo reminded himself, Jews still had no homeland from which to mobilize. They were a people of thought more than of guns.

In April of 1942, air raid sirens often wailed through Berlin. One Thursday night, Leo slipped into a churchyard; a metal box hidden there was the latest way station for the Lisbon mail drop. He left a partial manuscript in the box, chapters of a second book he'd begun in the past year. Entitled *Dieses Volk*, or *This People Israel*, the book was dedicated to Natalie. It depicted the soul, or mystical side, of Judaism reaching out to touch man with its moral message. A Christian friend, Baron von Veltheim, had asked Leo to let him safeguard the finished chapters. The baron put himself in jeopardy by helping a Jew, but he hadn't hesitated to do so.

Leaving the churchyard, Leo saw the streetlamps sharply dim and go out. A siren was blasting, warning the already bomb-damaged capital city into blackout. Above the swearing of Nazis at the corner, he could hear the distant buzz of Allied aircraft. He hurried across the Jewish section of tenements while someone called out to him; a hand at a window beckoned him toward a basement. Crouching down through a narrow doorway, he entered a darkened room topped by water pipes.

Names were whispered at him, identifying nine other Jews who occupied the clammy room. "Gestapo are upstairs," the occupants told him. "They put us here from our apartments. They sit in our rooms until the raid passes. If a bomb hits, they may escape. We, however, will scald to death from hot water in the exploding pipes."

Leo's eyes had grown accustomed to the darkness. On the floor, he glimpsed an old man crumpled into a bony heap. A yarmulke covered the man's head, grizzled sidecurls fell over his ears. "Herr Doktor Baeck," the man mumbled weakly. "I do not imagine you? They haven't taken you away? Every Friday, I came to your services. While I was young, Berlin was my joy. Now it is war and death."

Leo bent down beside the bony figure, wondering when the man had last eaten a good meal. Softly, he shared a few memories of Berlin synagogues, of classes Jews had attended at the university. War and prejudice, he said, were sacrilege. Fomented by human beings, they caused immense loss and destruction. But renewal would come—it must.

Suddenly, an explosion burst outside, shuddering in waves through the basement. The old man jerked upward, mouth agape and drooling, but Leo clasped the thin shoulders against him. As a wrinkled cheek grazed the yellow cloth star sewn months ago to his suit, Leo explained that a bomb had not hit the building. From his days as a *Feldrabbiner*, he'd learned the true sounds of a direct explosion. Perhaps, now, the night's bombing would stop. Perhaps a prayer should be said in unison—a prayer for sustenance in the "pestilence that walketh in darkness."

Glancing toward the clutch of Jews who had welcomed him off the street, Leo experienced a sense of pride, even of defiance. Pale and fuzzy in outline in the dimness was a series of other Jew stars sewn onto shirts and coats. The yellow cloth, meant to humiliate the Jews, was instead an illumination amidst the gloom. Stars, Leo told the nine Jews in the basement room as the air raid sirens abated, were fixed in the firmament of God, of the Lord is One. No star of Judaism, no matter how battered, would ever be wholly or permanently extinguished.

Just before dawn on the morning of January 27, 1943, Gestapo officers came for Leo. Prominent Jews in Germany were no longer spared.

Five days earlier, Leo had written to Ruth, Hermann, and Janne in England. He'd mentioned Hermann's accounting business and Ruth's welfare work; he'd congratulated Janne on her studies. Of himself, he said, "I am thankful when I can fulfill tasks and can be something to people and can give something to them. . . . The circle has narrowed. However, I [know] many loyalties from old friends."

On the morning of the twenty-seventh, he'd awakened, as usual, well before 5:00 A.M. His *tefillin* on, he offered a service. He was sipping a cup of coffee when the pounding began at his door. "Only the Gestapo," he'd say later, "would arrive at that hour."

He was to accompany the Nazi officers to a collection center on Grosse Hamburgerstrasse. He would be traveling by railway to Theresienstadt, the concentration camp in occupied Czechoslovakia. He could take a small suitcase, nothing more. The rest of his possessions must be left behind.

Curtly, Leo agreed to go. But he insisted on an hour to put everything in order. "You must come at once," he was told. "We've waited long enough to arrest you."

"One hour," Leo replied, standing firmly in the hall doorway. The tallest officer turned on his heels, grumbling that he would make a phone call outside. In ten minutes, when he returned, the man stomped past Leo into the parlor, kicking over an upholstered chair. "Orders are to wait an hour," he said. "You are still treated better, Herr Doktor, than you deserve."

At the desk where he'd listened to Hitler's Nuremberg Laws and had written his Yom Kippur sermon, Leo composed farewell notes to his family. He did not need to tell Ruth that three of his sisters had died in Theresienstadt. Sealing the envelopes, he placed them beside two postal orders to the gas and electric companies. No bills would be left unpaid. One of his co-workers had a key to the front door and directions to the Lisbon mail drop.

The notes and bills, Leo thought, would be posted. And what of the latest pages of *Dieses Volk*? He wrapped them in thick paper, sealing the edges with tape, and printed on a label: BARON VON VELTHEIM.

After the hour was over, Leo had packed his suitcase with clothes and *tallis, tefillin,* and prayer book. The Gestapo, planted like granite pillars in the doorway, glowered at him. "Whoever heard," one of them muttered, "of waiting for a Jew?"

He allowed himself only one backward glance. Already the apartment seemed distant from him. Was it here, he wondered, that students had gathered for *Shabbos* cakes and tea? Was it here that Natalie lit the Friday candles? On the credenza, shadows curled in overlapping pools; a brass floor lamp looked gray in the winter's bleakness. All the furniture, dishes, and accessories, except for the toppled armchair, were as Natalie had placed them. Yet Natalie was gone—and now he, too, must leave.

At the collection center, Leo's name was penciled on a list affixed to a wall. Dozens of Jews, hunched dismally over suitcases, were being processed for evacuation. The mere sight of Leo brought gasps, tears, and agonized moans. "No, no," voices rose. "Not Herr Doktor Baeck. Not the rabbi."

SS guards cocked their guns and barked out orders for silence. A young woman near the processing counter tried to stop crying, but sobs stuttered from her throat. Shoving Leo aside, a guard sauntered alongside the counter. As he reached the woman, he spun a shiny revolver in the air until he'd caught the barrel in his fingers. Abruptly then, he crashed the handle of the gun into the woman's breast. "Shut up, bitch!" he yelled as she fell, vomiting, to the floor.

Leo pressed forward to help the woman to her feet. Had a gun been in his own hand, he knew he'd have aimed it at the guard and pulled the trigger. Instead, opening his suit-

case, he took out a shirt to use as a bandage under the ooz-
ing circle of blood on the woman's dress. He was still
tending to her when an officer announced that the Theresienstadt transport would soon depart from Berlin's Anhalter
Station.

Theresienstadt, Leo explained carefully to the tearful young
woman, was the least harsh of the camps. It was built in
1789 as a military installation with several hundred houses,
two fortresses, and barracks. It functioned now as a ghetto
for privileged Jews—for medal winners and invalids of World
War I, for artists, for officials of the Reichsvereinigung, for
Jewish mates in mixed marriages. Leo told the woman that
she would recover there. Theresienstadt had medical rooms,
a bakery, a general store. Jewish musicians sent to the camp
could bring along their instruments.

The woman, eyes glazed with pain, leaned hopefully
toward Leo's words. "*Danke*, Herr Doktor Baeck," she said.
"Thank you. You are very kind."

Holding his suitcase in one hand, Leo led her gently past
several SS guards to a bench where she might rest. Nearby,
a policeman was tying tags stamped *Theresienstadt* onto a pile
of luggage. "And you, Herr Doktor Baeck," the woman said.
"Will you also sit down?"

Leo preferred to remain vigilant on his feet. He could not
take his eyes from the face of the Nazi guard who'd struck
the woman in the breast. Brutality, he saw, had settled into
the sneering mouth and slitted glance. Such a guard might
have caused the deaths in Theresienstadt of Leo's three sisters. Hitler's madness was a contagion to those he hired.

Six railway cars, announced an SS guard, were loading at
Anhalter Station. Lifting the injured woman from the bench,
Leo suddenly remembered the train from his childhood that
had rushed at him like a *golem*. He'd not run from that train
nor, at his Gymnasium graduation, from the stocking ball
plummeted into his hand. He had not, as a rabbi, fled Nazi
Germany. The monster he'd seen from his Berlin bedroom

had more than come true; the *golem* was alive in Nazi Germany. But even with untold cruelties and dangers lurking in Theresienstadt, Leo would not falter. Far greater forces existed in his world than either fear or foreboding.

10

Giving Hope Its Due

As Leo traveled in a "shipment" to Theresienstadt, thousands were cast into death camps in Poland. Hitler's war strategies may have been failing, but the führer had dominated Europe with his purge of Jews. From Rome, Athens, Budapest, and Vienna, from Paris, Warsaw, Munich, and Belgrade, Jews were evacuated to the camps. Nearly six million Jews would die in what historians would call the Holocaust—Hitler's systematic annihilation of huge numbers of the Jewish people. Nazi records would show that over one million dead Jews were children; that, in one twenty-four-hour period at Auschwitz, thirty-five thousand Jews were gassed and burned into ashes and chunks of bone. Essentially, the world at large allowed the Holocaust to happen, leaving Hitler free to commit history's most monstrous crime.

Arriving in Bohusovice, the nearest rail station to Theresienstadt, Leo's transport was searched for valuables—cig-

Above and opposite: A prisoner's sketches of Theresienstadt, where Baeck was sent after his arrest in 1943. Though Theresienstadt was the least harsh of the concentration camps, three of Baeck's sisters died there.

arettes, soap, cosmetics—then forced to march a mile in knee-high snow to the camp. In a stone admitting building, each arrival was assigned a number and a barracks. Married couples were separated; children over twelve could not live with either parent.

Stamped on Leo's records was the number 187984. He was pointed toward a large wooden barracks on a narrow street. Snow stuck like pockmarks to the slanting rooftops. The houses and barracks were originally built to hold no more than ten thousand inhabitants. Now they teemed with sixty thousand Jews.

Three children and two other men from Leo's transport were assigned with him to the barracks where he opened the door. The children pushed against him, quivering, for

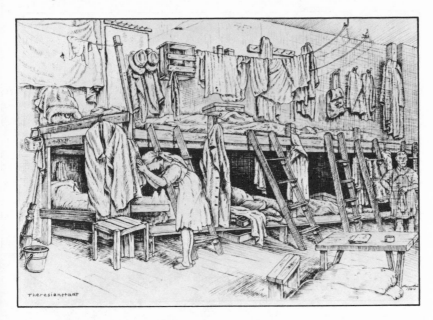

protection. Inside, reeking of urine, rows of filthy wooden bunks rose in four and five decks with so little overhead space that inmates had to lean forward when sitting. Crunched everywhere were people, emaciated and bruised. Six little boys stood listlessly in a line of inmates by a latrine, pants stained from waiting. "Dysentery," one of the men rasped to Leo. "It spreads through the camps, and no one can retain food. At least, Herr Doktor, we aren't in Auschwitz. Numbers are tattooed there, I hear, onto forearms."

On his first night in Theresienstadt, Leo went from barracks to barracks. Inmates recognized him, grabbing his lapels, pulling him toward their bunks, asking of family in Germany. He found a pail for water and bathed feverish faces. He spoke of Jews he knew who were left in the Reich and of those he'd seen on transports at the deportation center.

By morning, his eyes were reddened from fatigue and from the stench of human excrement in the barracks. A guard or-

Leo administering to a fellow prisoner, as depicted by artist Karl Godwin

dered him at gunpoint to the admitting building for permanent work assignment at the camp.

"Garbage collector," the guard sneered. "We've found you, Herr Rabbi, a fitting occupation—much like what you've always done by guiding your Jews."

Leo and another inmate were strapped to a heavy wagon and sent on a route across the camp. At each barracks, prisoners stumbled outside, silently dumping garbage and dead vermin into the wagon. Yet on his second day at the assignment, his shoulders rubbed raw from the leather straps, Leo was deep in conversation. The inmate bound next to him was interested in philosophy. At day's end, while the two men dropped bags of decaying rats into a truck routed to an outside dump, they were seriously discussing Kant, Spinoza, and Hegel.

Theresienstadt was not a gas-and-oven killing center, but it dealt in death. When Leo went at night to visit other barracks, he found the Jews despondent and ill. Disease, starvation, and physical torture were rampant. Nazi "sanitation crews" unloaded the dead and dying from "funeral" trucks into pits. Babies, still breathing, were crushed under the weight of bodies. Straining past drab gray buildings in the center square, Leo and his fellow garbage hauler could see the trucks roll by. "Someday," Leo said, "someday the horror will stop."

Hitler had designated Theresienstadt as a model camp, plotting to keep the International Red Cross, a worldwide welfare organization, from guessing his Final Solution. During Leo's imprisonment, Red Cross officials were invited on a camp tour. In preparation, Nazis herded thousands of the sickest Jews onto lofts in the barracks, leaving lower floors less crowded. Children, beaten and threatened with the death of parents, were ordered to play happily in the streets or to sit at hastily built playgrounds with Jewish "teachers," drawing pictures or writing poems. Leo refused to participate in the charade; he was kept alive to add to the false image of the camp. Later, he remarked that the Red Cross hadn't truly bothered to investigate Theresienstadt. The tour was made from an open car; no official climbed the stairs of any barracks to discover the rows of spittle- and urine-covered Jews.

Survivors of Theresienstadt would remember Leo's kindness and strength. Whatever his aches or pains, he provided others with a precious spiritual security. "The soul and the hour," he'd tell the inmates, "meet each other. What is given to us, we have to do." After the war, he described a need for patience and imagination to surmount catastrophe. Patience, he said, was the "power of resilience that did not let the will to live give way." Imagination was a "vision that ever again and in spite of everything makes . . . [one] see a future."

The months of 1943 dragged by in the grime and death of Theresienstadt, marked by the arrival of new transports and by outgoing shipments "east." Behind the Nazis' backs, Leo organized a skilled team of prisoners to nurse a typhus epidemic. His own seventieth birthday passed in the camp, but no one thought of him as old. Though he subsisted on watery soup and potato skins, he still walked briskly and with dignity. In stolen moments, he scribbled new paragraphs of *This People Israel* on scraps of paper, hiding them beneath a loosened floorboard at his bunk.

Leo's riskiest act in the winter of 1943 was to create a secret lecture series. From a chilly barracks loft, he spoke in the middle of the night of Plato and Maimonides to battered and shivering Jews. For weeks, the appointed hour of each lecture was a password exchanged between barracks. On the appointed night, dozens of inmates crept between buildings and up a stairway to the unheated loft. Some could barely stand; beatings and illnesses had crippled or weakened them. Yet the chance to hear the Rabbi Baeck, who'd memorized Plato in Greek, who'd written his famous Yom Kippur sermon and his more famous book, was a balm to their wounds. For an hour or more, the Jews of Theresienstadt—like Jews since their beginnings—forgot their sorrow and pain in the glorious gift of words.

Leo was imprisoned in Theresienstadt for twenty-eight months. His lectures were never invaded by Nazis, but he saw at least a hundred dead bodies a day loaded onto the trucks that sped into the fields. He listened to the screams of Jews tortured in a nearby fortress. Punishments were meted out at the slightest provocation. Stealing a scrap of potato could mean weeks of beatings in a clammy cell. Inmates who stumbled in the street, sniffled, or spit blood might be kicked into unconsciousness. A man accused of keeping cigarettes was seared in the eyes with a red-hot poker. In March 1943, sixteen Jews were hanged—one for sending a simple love note to his wife.

Outward defiance at the camp was the most certain path

to death. Yet Leo had fewer and fewer compunctions about preserving his own safety. When a young man and wife conceived a child at Theresienstadt, the Nazis ordered an abortion. By then, the wife was in her eighth month of pregnancy. Leo announced to Nazi officials that abortion at so late a stage would kill the woman as well as the child. He requested that Frau Groag be able to complete her pregnancy. With no reply given him, and with Frau Groag dragged from her barracks, he managed to unstrap himself from his garbage wagon. He grabbed the confused and frightened husband and ran to the rooms used for surgery. Frau Groag, legs tied apart, lay drugged and trembling on a cot. "Your husband waits outside," Leo said. "We are taking you back to the barracks."

"I want to have my baby, Herr Doktor Baeck," Frau Groag murmured.

"A Sabbath child you'll have," Leo answered.

Frau Groag's child was born on a Friday afternoon, just one hour before *Shabbos* sundown. At a previous meeting with the camp commandant, Leo had used the last of his influence as a prominent person to win a reprieve from suffocation for the Groag baby.

What he and the commandant did not know, however, was that most of the outside world believed Leo to be dead. Germany's Adolf Eichmann, newest overseer of Hitler's purge, had ordered the liquidation of Herr Doktor Leo Baeck. Only a coincidence had kept Leo alive. A Moravian rabbi named Beck died in Theresienstadt. Reading the name on the camp death rolls, Eichmann had mistaken the dead rabbi for Leo and publicized the news.

Over a year passed before Leo learned of Eichmann's error. Resisters, darting out of the forests, had smuggled information to him past the camp gates. Under the same loose floorboard that covered his manuscript, he hid various bits of the information, especially foreign newspaper articles tracking Allied victories and German defeats. World War II, the reports said, was definitely drawing toward an end. Yet

Spared by chance from Adolf Eichmann's order for his death,
Baeck survived more than two years at Theresienstadt.

in August of 1943, a Czechoslovakian laborer crawled into
Theresienstadt to tell Leo the truth of Auschwitz and other
killing centers. Gas pellets, said the tearful man, were released into newly constructed "medicinal shower stalls" at
the camps. Trainloads of Jews were told to breathe deeply
in the showers to cleanse themselves. Once the doors were
bolted shut, helpless men, women, and children burst their
lungs trying to breathe. In their final moments of agony,
some embraced each other in love and recited the *Shema*.

"All day and night," wept the laborer, "chimneys belch
the smoke and stench of human bodies. Nazis plant trees
and flowers around Auschwitz's ovens. They trick Allied
aircraft flying over the camp. Many of the dead, Herr Doktor Baeck, are from Theresienstadt transports. Please do what
you wish with what I've told you."

All that August, as Leo strained at his daily garbage rounds
under swarms of ravenous flies, he was unusually quiet. His
companion, accustomed to the philosophy debates that were

a diversion against pain, worried over Leo's health. But what troubled Leo was not physical. His own internal debate concerned telling the Jews of Theresienstadt about Auschwitz's gas chambers. Did he owe his fellow inmates the facts? he wondered. Would describing the "showers" provide anything but an expectation of death? Besides, if the war ended soon, wouldn't Jews left in the camp be free of the Nazi transports?

One midnight, during one of his lectures on the now sweltering loft, Leo found himself imagining a lushly flowered meadow. Images of violets and nasturtiums seized his thoughts. He could almost erase the odor of urine and pus-filled flesh and smell the blossoms. He was not certain, of course, whether he would survive the Nazis to see another meadow, but hope persisted—just as he hoped to see Ruth, Hermann, and Janne. Gazing at the Jews propped up against the rafters, he suddenly shook his head. He would say nothing of Auschwitz. He would not voluntarily destroy remnants of hope. Man's cruelty toward man had reached insane and ghastly proportions in Adolf Hitler's Germany. To counter this, patience and imagination, strength of will and a hopeful vision, must be preserved.

Drenched with perspiration, Leo waited on the loft long after his audience had tiptoed back to their quarters. The *tallis* he'd brought with him to Theresienstadt, along with *tefillin* and prayer book, had been cut up with knives, but he lifted his shoulders as if he were wrapping the shawl over him. The meadow pictured in his mind floated onto childhood memories of his family, of the elders scolding him when he'd dreamed of knowledge beyond Torah and Talmud, of his pulpits in Oppeln, Düsseldorf, Berlin. He realized he would have to answer for hiding the truth of Auschwitz. He would have to bear the possibility that his decision was wrong. Certain people would accuse him of playing God with the Jews. Others might say he did owe the truth, that even suicides caused by that truth were a private and personal choice.

A gunshot sounded outside the wooden barracks, followed by a tormented shriek. Leo breathed in the grief of another death. No, he mouthed in answer to the rancid darkness, death would be opposed by hope. Eventually, when Judaism's story was uncovered in all its detail, human beings everywhere would need to examine the humanity of their own souls. For the moment, however, he'd bury the story of Auschwitz and give hope its due. Past each death shriek, he thought, might rise a chant of joy. Past each trial and tribulation could lay a more lasting repose.

11

The Most Difficult Renewal

On the seventh of May 1945, the German nation surrendered unconditionally to the Allied powers. The formality was not witnessed by Adolf Hitler. A week before, the führer had committed suicide in his underground bunker in Berlin. In his last statement, he raged that the Jews—not he—caused the war. He exhorted the new leaders of Germany to "uphold the racial laws."

Russian troops, liberating towns in their rush across the Reich, poured victoriously into Theresienstadt. Already, the Nazis had fled. Fluttering to the ground in their wake were leaflets, which had been dropped by American planes, promising help. The stronger inmates painted over swastikas on barracks and tore the yellow stars from clothing. "Say a blessing for us, Herr Doktor Baeck," a young man called to Leo in the center square. Smiling, straps to his garbage wagon set aside, Leo waved a hand upward.

Had Hitler's twelve-year regime toppled? Was freedom a

wish come true? Jews who could walk, or even crawl, gathered in Theresienstadt's streets. Skeletal in appearance, they leaned on one another, wept, tried to believe. A girl, arms like bony sticks, tilted toward Leo in bewilderment. Could everyone leave the camp? she asked. Would there be shelter? Had the Nazis truly disappeared?

The hurting was over, Leo answered. In February, the camp children—scarcely a hundred survived of the fifteen thousand sent to Theresienstadt—thought he was leaving them. Twelve hundred Jews had been released that month from the camp, a "goodwill gesture" from the teetering Nazis. Leo was among the discharged, but as always he refused escape. Now, liberation would save the children from having to hear, while imprisoned, stories of ovens and human smoke.

Along with the Russians, the Red Cross entered Theresienstadt, bringing food and medical supplies. Nazis had tried to dynamite evidence of gas chambers and, retreating across Germany, had shifted prisoners from camps near Allied battalions to those in outlying zones. Thousands of Jewish children, skin like thin paste over rib cages and spines, were marched into the countryside—just days before liberation— and buried alive. Trainloads of the desperately ill were relocated to Theresienstadt; only thirty thousand Jews survived of the one hundred seventy thousand there in a five-year count.

Finding typhus symptoms in the new arrivals, Leo set up a quarantine barracks. Inmates and the Red Cross had asked him to help run the camp, and he posted guidelines. Observation of the Quarantine Rules Is Necessary, he'd printed on a sign. Help Us With Our Work; the Return Home Shall Be Made Possible.

Many stricken Jews weren't willing to be quarantined. Trusting no one, more primitive than civilized in their starved, tortured state, they wanted to run free. "Let us out!" they yelled. "Hitler is dead! The war is over!"

Calmly, Leo cleaned their wounds of maggots. He bargained with the ill, promising to sleep alongside them in the quarantine barracks until shelter outside the camp was arranged. He would trade the risk of contracting typhus, he said, for the willingness of those who were ill to stay temporarily confined.

Feeling a touch of his hand on their foreheads, the disease-infested Jews suddenly remembered the Chief Rabbi of Berlin. It was Herr Doktor Baeck who had represented them to the Nazis. It was he who'd urged them to leave Germany while he remained, who'd badgered officials for visas and aided resisters, who'd spirited children to safety and helped many cross borders. It was the Rabbi Leo Baeck, son of Samuel Bäck, who'd preached Torah at synagogues until *Kristallnacht*, who'd written so proudly of Judaism to both Christians and Jews. How could the Jews under quarantine refuse his request? How could they not agree?

In the first weeks of liberation, Leo assisted the Red Cross in treating the typhus. Displaced-persons camps opened across Europe, providing lodging and food for war refugees, but active typhus cases weren't admitted. Leo wrote reunion letters for Jews whose relatives had settled outside the Reich. For those who didn't know if family members were alive, he placed hundreds of phone calls to persons who might begin searches. Making contacts, however, was difficult. Large parts of Europe had been gutted by the war. Bombed-out cities were without telephone service; homes and apartments might no longer exist.

In mid-May, Major Patrick Dolan of the United States Army traveled from Prague to rescue Leo—described to him as "the pope of the German Jews." Jewish leaders in England and America, discovering that Leo was alive in Theresienstadt, had persuaded the American Office of Strategic Services to dispatch an emissary to the camp. Major Dolan was to fly his charge to Paris to obtain necessary papers and to board a connecting flight to England. But Patrick Dolan did not

expect to have to wait nearly two months before the tall,
white-haired rabbi of renown would accompany him. "I re-
gret the delay," Leo said. "If your orders permit, Major Dolan, return to Prague. I will stay in Theresienstadt until every
Jew has a destination."

Through the month of June, Europe's concentration camps
emptied. Gas ovens were laid bare by American troops, along
with storerooms of gold inlays, human hair, and soap made
of human fat. The Allies participated in occupying Germany to disarm its bases of military power. Most German
Jews, no matter what protection they might receive in the
future from a newly elected government, would not resettle
in Germany. The people of Deutschland had sacrificed them;
Nazism reeked for them from the soil. Leo's letter writing
continued. He sent introductory notes to his friends and
colleagues in various countries to introduce Jewish refugees
who wanted to begin a new life.

Gradually, Jews left Theresienstadt. Some inmates had
been transferred to displaced-persons camps, others to Russian hospitals. Large numbers flew to America, England, or
Palestine; thousands more hiked or jumped trains or hay-
wagons to hunt in agony for living relatives. On July 1, 1945,
Leo at last left the concentration camp with Major Dolan. In
an army jeep, fueled at a pump near Leo's old garbage wagon, the two men drove to an airport near Prague to board
a U.S. Flying Fortress for Paris. A telegram was sent to Hermann Berlak in London, announcing the Rabbi Baeck's arrival. An American soldier escorted Leo up the steps to the
plane, welcoming him to life beyond Theresienstadt with a
salute and a stick of chewing gum.

The Flying Fortress set a straight course from Prague to
Paris. At a window, his scraps of book chapters retrieved
from the barracks floorboard and packed in a suitcase, Leo
focused on the plane's passage over the Rhine River, following the stout line of blue as it narrowed to a tapering
matchstick in the view from the plane. He was fifty pounds

lighter than on the morning he'd left his Germany of early dreams for Theresienstadt's gates. Along with Natalie, Otto Hirsch, and three sisters, another of his sisters had died of Nazism. Was God in the concentration camps? Leo had been asked. Where was God when the Jews needed Him? God, Leo had replied, entered wherever He was invited—His sustenance of spirit filling the deepest hell, lighting the blackest pit.

Yet it was man, Leo said, who must do the inviting. Man must choose between good and evil, act in mercy or in corruption. With the chewing gum soft in his mouth, the plane engines roaring toward freedom, Leo prayed silently for the latest and most difficult renewal of his people Israel. Remembering the birth in Theresienstadt of Frau Groag's blessed *Shabbos kind*—Sabbath child, he turned to Patrick Dolan, who sat beside him. "The triumph of the Jews, Major," he said with conviction, "is that out of the ashes of death, they eternally renew themselves; out of the ancient covenant, they still reach for God's hand."

Leo would not destroy his yellow star. Frayed at the edges, faded into paleness, it represented dignity to him in the face of outrage. In London, reunited with Ruth, Hermann, and Janne, he kept the star between pages of a prayer book. Having possessions again—*tallis, tefillin*, sacred books— seemed unreal. Were twenty-eight months in Theresienstadt more real? Writing of the camp, he said, "Before me so often appear the shadows, the shadows of those who died and the shadows of those who led them to their deaths. . . . Perhaps the healing process sometimes lasts as long as the illness."

Letters that reached Leo in England, or people who flocked to him, asked in dread of their loved ones. While Ruth baked pies and cakes for her father, he wrote or spoke of the dead. *Our dear friend,* he said in one note, . . . *was sent to the east in the fall of 1942, to my great pain.* In another letter, referring to a woman inmate of Theresienstadt who'd been shipped by cattle car to Auschwitz, he wrote carefully, *I suspect she was on one of the numerous transports that were sent to the east.*

The postwar welfare of European Jews became Leo's great concern. His days were as busy with responsibilities as when he'd lived in Berlin. "Grandfather, you must rest," twenty-year-old Janne insisted, but at seventy-three he felt pressed for time. He was asked to head various organizations. Elected president of England's Council for the Protection of the Rights and Interests of the Jews from Germany, he also headed the World Union for Progressive Judaism and the Society for Jewish Study. The Society gave lectures similar to those on the old Hochschule curriculum. Voice hoarse with memories of his fellow garbage hauler at Theresienstadt, Leo would address war survivors with his love of theology and philosophy. "People listened," said a friend from Germany, "to the man who impressed everyone."

In January 1947, Leo was invited to the United States by the Union of American Hebrew Congregations, a reform, or liberal, branch of Judaism. Entertained by President Harry Truman in the White House, who vowed more visas for refugees, he was the first foreign clergyman to present opening prayer in the House of Representatives. The United States, in 1944, had ignored eyewitness accounts of Auschwitz from several escapees, refusing to search out gas chambers and ovens. Sensing America's guilt feelings toward Jews, Leo's prayer at the House of Representatives implored God's guidance "that we may not evade history, but we may be granted history."

Sight-seeing in Washington and New York, he began hearing the word *Holocaust.* Sometimes he was stared at for telltale marks or scars. Congregants of synagogues, receiving photographs from secret Nazi files, apologized to him for faring better than Europe's Jews. Overwhelmed, Americans viewed pictures of emaciated bodies piled in mass graves; of ragged, bloody limbs torn from babies' sockets; of the ghastly results of camp medical experiments that left men castrated and women breastless.

"Will you ever forgive the Germans?" Leo was asked.

"I forgive the Germans?" he said. "It is for the Germans to forgive themselves."

War trials held in Nuremberg, Germany, riveted world attention on the Holocaust. Thousands of lesser officials of the German death machine would not be indicted, but the Allies decided to try major instigators for their crimes against humanity. The first trial, beginning late in 1945 and ending in October 1946, consisted of testimony before an international military tribunal. Twelve of the defendants were sentenced to death, three to life imprisonment, four to shorter terms; three others were acquitted. U.S. Chief Prosecutor Robert H. Jackson commented that the world had never known "slaughter on such a scale." If the causes of Nazi Germany weren't eliminated, he said, "it is not an irresponsible prophecy to say that the twentieth century may yet succeed in bringing the doom of civilization."

Leo was the first prominent German Jew to make a return trip to Germany. He contacted Jewish families who had resettled among the war debris, offering them international welfare assistance. To the neediest families, he turned over payments he'd received from his book royalties. He bought food for Christians who were punished for befriending Jews during the war, and he visited his old friend Baron von Veltheim. Tenderly, the baron relinquished the early chapters of *This People Israel*. "You are finishing the manuscript?" the baron asked.

"Yes," Leo said. "The story of the Jews must be told."

In 1948, Leo was offered a six-month annual post as visiting professor at Hebrew Union College in Cincinnati, Ohio. He accepted the offer, planning to bring Janne with him to the United States. The college was perched on a hill surrounded by sloping meadows. "A beautiful place to teach

After the end of World War II, Baeck traveled frequently in
the United States, where he met with notables such as hu-
manitarian Albert Schweitzer *(above)* and philosopher Martin
Buber *(below)*.

midrash," he told Janne. "In Theresienstadt, I hungered for the sight of a meadow."

Each year, he traveled to Cincinnati. By 1950, he was a British citizen living in London, but again he visited Germany. Preaching at a new Berlin synagogue, he spoke of the once flourishing German Jews. Their yearning for the things of mind and spirit, he said, sparked the emergence in Europe of not only Freud, Marx, and Einstein, but of a whole roster of Jewish achievers in humane and cultural endeavors. To cherish such creators and their achievements was the "task of all Jews everywhere."

If Leo was growing tired, he confided his fatigue to no one, always doing what remained to be done. In 1948, in a landmark decision, the United Nations partitioned Palestine into separate Jewish and Arab states. The new Jewish state of Israel—finally a reclaimed homeland—triumphantly granted citizenship to Jews seeking residence. Its arid land would be irrigated by eager settlers. Yet seven Arab states invaded Israel in May 1948. Despite a belated world outcry against bloodshed, anti-Semitism still simmered. If man's conscience, Leo preached in Cincinnati and London, weren't roused, prejudice toward any people might lead to the violence and terror of another Holocaust.

This People Israel, Leo's second book, was completed in October of 1956. The meaning of being Jewish, Leo had written, was to teach the belief in one God, the honoring of justice, and the value of the individual. *Every man is a world in himself*, he wrote. *The miracle of morality makes him truly man.*

The fatigue that he had been feeling had not, however, receded. In late October 1956, Leo was suddenly hospitalized in London for intestinal cancer. His family hovered over him, but he would talk to them of little except their own futures. So many millions, he said, had died before him; he'd walked with death in many garbs. Only when he was too weak from lost blood to converse at length did he tell Ruth, "I will soon join your mother—and all the people of Torah and Talmud devoured by persecution. None of us really relinquishes loved ones who wait behind. How well I've learned that life, even with its pauses, is a continuum."

"Yes, Papa," Ruth had whispered, wrapping Leo's *tallis* around his shoulders, smoothing the fringes over the bed sheet. "Truly you have taught our people of history and eternity. You have been our *Seelsorger*, one who cares for our souls."

On November 2, 1956, Leo smiled up at Janne and Hermann, clasped Ruth's hand, and at the age of eighty-three, gently closed his eyes. His risk taking, forged in Nazi Germany out of a scholar's mind and temperament, was ended; sermons and writings would have to carry his message. His death was announced in headlines throughout Europe and America. Telegrams of condolence poured into the Berlak home; contributions to Jewish causes were pledged in Leo's name. A tombstone, purchased for his gravesite in London, would carry Hebrew words that he'd requested—marking the special heritage he shared with his father, grandfather, and great-grandfather. Translated, the words read: A DESCENDANT OF RABBIS.

Honors and eulogies accumulated. Leo was, said one tribute, "a man who drew his full strength from his living belief in God and from his impassioned love for the Jewish people." In Berlin, the new German government issued a postage stamp with his picture on it and named a street for him. His books were quickly translated into various languages, reprinted in expensive editions, and published in paperback.

What might have most pleased Leo were acts honoring the creative and spiritual scholarship of the German Jews. Three Leo Baeck Institutes, dedicated to collecting memorabilia of German Jewish history, opened in New York, London, and Jerusalem. A Leo Baeck School in Haifa, Israel, gained immediate recognition for high educational standards; Leo Baeck College in London would train Reform

Leo Baeck, a descendant of rabbis

rabbis in Leo's liberal approach to Judaism. His steady but determined constancy during the Holocaust prompted a California congregation to call itself the Leo Baeck Temple.

To those who had met Leo or read his works, he signified religion put into action. History had confronted this "descendant of rabbis" with the need to preach and to enact his ideas in the face of wholesale death and defamation. Under circumstances of starkest adversity, he taught that living itself was a Commandment. His words, echoing against present-day world stockpiles of guns, bombs, and missiles—against wars for survival Israel has fought since 1948— are commemorated in hundreds of books and harrowing exhibits concerning World War II.

On a street in today's East Berlin, the front wall of a synagogue burned on *Kristallnacht* is preserved as a reminder of Adolf Hitler's Germany. A plaque, placed there by a slowly rebuilding Berlin Jewish community, reads *Vergesst es nie*— It must never be forgotten. The Holocaust, Leo told us, put our morality at stake. It showed that man, without decency or compassion, is capable of committing unbelievable harm. Remembering the Holocaust in a world still torn by hatreds, by ever-growing possibilities of self-destruction, is to think of what being human means. And remembering the Rabbi Leo Baeck is to celebrate one man's valor and devotion in behalf of his long-suffering but undaunted people.

Books for Further Reading

Baeck, Leo. *The Essence of Judaism.* Edited and revised by I. Howe, based on the translation from the German by V. Grubenweiser and L. Pearl (London, 1936). New York: Schocken Books, 1948.

——. *Judaism and Christianity: Essays.* Philadelphia: The Jewish Publication Society of America, 1958.

——. "In Memory of Two of Our Dead." In *Year Book I.* New York: East & West Library for the Leo Baeck Institute, 1956.

——. *This People Israel: The Meaning of Jewish Existence.* Translated by Albert H. Friedlander. Philadelphia: The Jewish Publication Society of America, 1965.

Baker, Leonard. *Days of Sorrow and Pain: Leo Baeck and the Berlin Jews.* New York: Macmillan Publishing Co., 1978.

Friedlander, Albert H. *Out of the Whirlwind: A Reader of Holocaust Literature.* New York: Union of American Hebrew Congregations, 1968.

Meltzer, Milton. *Never to Forget: The Jews of the Holocaust.* New York: Harper & Row, 1976.

Stadtler, Bea. *The Holocaust: A History of Courage and Resistance.* New York: Behrman House, 1974.

Swarsensky, Manfred E. *Intimates and Ultimates.* Madison, Wis.: Edgewood College, 1981.

Index

Page numbers in *italics* refer to captions.

Bäck, Samuel (father), 1, 7, 11,
    14, 17, 18, 20, 42
  death of, 25–26, 69
  education of, 2
  stories told by, 4–5, 41
  as writer, 3
Baden-Baden, 53
Baeck, Leo:
  admiration of, 18–19, 21, 28,
    32, 34, 37, 84, 91–92, 94,
    98–100
  Auschwitz, knowledge of
    extermination at, 86–88
  Bar Mitzvah of, 5, 17
  in Berlin, 7–11, 8, 13–15, 21,
    24, 28–56, 60–61, 64–69,
    71–77
  Berlin apartment of, 29, 31,
    76
  books written by, 18, 29, 32,
    73, 76, 84, 92, 95, 97, 98
  on Christians who helped
    Jews, 54, 62
  in Cincinnati, 95, 97
  death of, 97–98
  in Düsseldorf, 19–20
  Eichmann's order for death
    of, 85, 86
  emigration of Jews arranged
    by, 64–65
  escapes for Jews arranged
    by, 51–52, 60, 72
  essays written by, 13, 18
  on faith, 40
  family name of, 1, 5
  father's coat worn by, 1, 2,
    3–4, 6
  as Feldrabbiner, 24–27, 25, 60,
    74
  on forgiving the Germans, 95
  formal statement to German
    Jews issued by, 39

Baeck, Leo, cont'd.
  in France, 24
  on freedom, 39
  graduation from Gymna-
    sium school by, 1–4, 6
  in Hamburg, 62–64
  at Hochschule seminary, 7,
    8, 9, 21, 24, 29, 30, 32, 36,
    51, 66
  on imagination, 83
  international recognition of,
    32, 34, 44, 91–92, 94, 98–
    100
  in jail, 43–44
  on Judaism vs. Christianity,
    18
  on Kristallnacht, 52–58
  letter written to Hitler by, 36,
    38–39
  in Lissa, 1–6
  in London, 93, 97
  on meaning of being Jew-
    ish, 97
  in Oppeln, 11–13, 16–19
  Oppeln apartment of, 17, 18
  ordination of, 11
  organizations joined by, 28–
    29, 37, 94
  on patience, 83
  postwar visits to Germany
    of, 95, 97
  poverty of, 2, 9–10
  as president of Reichsver-
    tretung, 37, 39, 41, 60, 64,
    67
  rabbinical studies of, 7–11,
    12
  sermons of, 19, 27, 41–44
  sisters and brothers of, 1, 19,
    26, 42, 75, 93
  in Switzerland, 47
  Talmud studied by, 2, 5, 9

About the Author

"Leo Baeck saw both Judaism and life itself as a continuum," says author ANNE E. NEIMARK. "I hope to reach young readers with this viewpoint. Rabbi Baeck learned that, to survive catastrophe, one must nurture both patience and imagination. All human beings can gain from considering his insights."

Mrs. Neimark has written five other young-adult biographies, all well received, on subjects including Louis Braille, Sigmund Freud, and Thomas Gallaudet. She and her husband have two sons and a daughter. A native of Chicago, Mrs. Neimark lives in Highland Park, Illinois.